# WOULD YOU LIKE FRIES

# WITH THAT?

*A SATIRICAL GUIDE TO
NAVIGATING THE
CUSTOMER/FOOD SERVICE INDUSTRY.*

## MARIAH LYNDE

Copyright © 2024 Mariah Lynde
Publisher Fae Corps LLC

All rights reserved. This book or any portion thereof may not be reproduced or used in any manner whatsoever without the express written permission of the publisher except for the use of brief quotations in a book review.

This is a work of fiction, any references to historical events, real people, or real places are used fictitiously. Names, characters, and places are products of the author's imagination.

Fae Corps LLC
5415 Raven Dr
Charleston WV 25306
Faecorpspublishing.org

# CHAPTER 1
## PREFACE

I want to be very clear, this book started as a way to keep my sanity. While still trying to focus on writing as a career, there was no escaping the fact I needed to find a job to work to pay my bills, take care of my family, etc. I fell into the same ago old trap – I'd find a temporary job and write in my spare time.

Since the day I made that fateful decision, my writing career had ground to a halt. The lofty goals and dreams I had, were no longer within my capability.

After a lengthy absence from the American workforce, I no longer held the licenses and registrations required of my chosen profession. So when I returned to the daily grind, I found myself seeking jobs at minimum wage with the thought I would get something better later, or that my writing career would take off.

Imagine my surprise when the only place to give me a shot, was as delivery driver in the good service industry. Fast forward roughly five years, and it feels like a lifetime. There was no magically better job at the end of the rainbow. No better salary or a plethora of time to sit down and write out the next Vengeance of Avalon novel.

No.

What I received was a steady paycheck, a string of migraines, and a heap of worry that causes me to panic anytime a phone rings more than twice. I still work in food service, no longer a delivery driver, but a manager.

Allow me to tell you, that if you though working in the emergency medical field could make you doubt humanity, it pales in comparison to the dregs of society you see when working in food service. The last five years have honestly had a detrimental effect to my belief in the general good of people. COVID notwithstanding, there had been a fundamental lack of general grace and civility that has caused me to witness first hand some of the most ridiculous idiocy you can imagine.

That is not to say it's been all bad. Far from it, but more often than not lately, it seems like a steady stream of the inconceivable and downright asinine. So, as one does, there are nights were coworkers and I blow off steam over a few brews, or a good meal. If we can manage to arrange having the same day off, of course. In training them, or giving instances of scenarios, we have shared stories from the battlefield as it were.

When it came to the subject of my abandoned writing, I was asked what the problem was. Surprised at the interest, I had answered truthfully. It is hard to force your brain to create and detail your fantasy world of make believe when you are mired in thoughts of dealing with a problem customer, or some incident that happened with a coworker trying to cause a problem. There were some healthy references to other managerial protocols that aren't really important, but needless to say, I outlined the fact that instead of being able to relax and take time to write what I wanted to write – I was living in the workplace even when I wasn't there.

So then, they asked if it would help if I just started bleeding out some of my thoughts about work on the page to just get rid of it. Not a bad idea. I'm a writer, we fixate. And fixate. And then fixate some more until we remember what the point of it all was in the first place.

So, the general piecing together began. Small snippets of incidents, customer and employee included began to bleed onto the computer screen. Did it help with the fantasy writer's block? Not a bit, but I no longer feel like my brain is going to explode and I am producing words of some sort. Sharing my experience and mind with the world at large. So that's something, right?

Do I hope one day I will find the time and ability to separate work and home so I can return to the fantasy place of my dreams and write that world? Absolutely. Sadly, that day is not today, but I can give you this book compiled of situations and scenarios that I have encountered repeatedly in the last five years.

For some, this book will be funny because they had worked in some form of customer service and recognize the scenario. Others, will find it humorous and believe it is an exaggeration of events just intended to bring laughter to the world. Then, there will be others, who consider my work trash and tawdry, in no way accurate. Pretty sure you realize, they will say such because I struck a nerve about something.

What I want you to do, my dear reader, is just take this for what it is. Stories, and quips. Words on a page. Something intended to bring some form of enjoyment to your life. Whether it's in solidarity, or the idea that this is more woo-joo fantasy writing. Your choice.

That said, Let the games begin.

## CHAPTER 2
## INTRODUCTION AND EXPLANATION
## – A WARNING

Customer Service is a field that is tantamount to fighting dragons. This is not an exaggeration. Everyday is filled with people outside of your home setting, in a society that is constantly recording your every move. As if that were not enough, you also have to follow the strictures of the company you work for, by only using acceptable practices to de-escalate situations as they arise.

This means, that if someone comes in and yells at you, to your face – you have to smile and apologize. Even if, you did nothing wrong. Even if, after looking further into the matter you realize it is a scam.

Allow me to say, it does not matter where you are in the Customer/Food service industry. You could be the lowliest hourly worker or the district manager of a franchise chain but the amount of pure vitriol you receive from the populace is tantamount to seeing a nuclear fallout. People long ago forgot manners and general niceties, the grand movement of my childhood that proclaimed "the customer is always right" bred a sense of pure entitlement and meanness that is unparalleled.

This book, is about to explore all of that. Now, before anyone gets too worked up, please keep in mind – not all of this is about customers. It is also about the types of staff and workers you will encounter in these places. Not all of them are bad, some of them are pleasant memories that you look back on with fondness because of how amusing they were.

True, these pale in comparison to the vivid recollections of the horror stories, but they do exist. With that in mind, please remember that any preconceived notions that one has over people that work in food service or customer service, should be checked at the door. Coming in to this with an open mind, makes these stories or characters more relatable.

Now, please note all names and places as well as some events, were renamed to protect the innocent and not-so-innocent. Hopefully, by the end of this, anyone still in Customer Service Jobs has a laugh or a new way to cope with the situations they face on a daily basis. Anyone not in these jobs, may have a better understanding of just what these workers go through and take a little pity on those who do so.

Not every chapter of this book will be about people or sticky situations that they can find themselves in. There will also be chapters that underline specific items or techniques that are required in the world of customer service, whether it be in goods to be acquired or food service. There are several specific principals which govern the whole of the service industry no matter where you find yourself. So these particulars will be explained in further detail for those that are just beginning their work in customer service and considering moving up the ladder, or for the customers who are not aware of these principles and why some workers respond in the way they do.

This book, while satirical in nature, holds true to one key principle. You have to be able to laugh at life. Sometimes, no matter how bad it is, the ability to find humor in the situation is what makes a person stronger and able to move forward from it.

With that in mind, let us begin the journey.

## **CHAPTER 3**
## **ARROGANT ANDY**

There is no single category for the Arrogant Andy. These people exist as both customers and co-workers. Sadly, no matter which side they are on, they prove to be a migraine inducing experience.

This is not to say that in some scenarios they are not right to be arrogant. By all means, if you are a doctor and you save lives, yeah! You are right to know you are a rock star! You help people, you save lives. By all means, own who you are...however, there is a line where it becomes a little too pervasive. The best people, the ones secure in their skill and ability, do so with a small sense of decorum. They do not use their knowledge and accomplishments to try and one up others in any scenario.

That said, in this chapter we will explore the Arrogant Andy as both a customer and a co-worker. I feel it is only fair to represent both sides as two such similar people on both sides can cause a scenario to quickly unravel.

Our example brings us to a Friday night in a mid-size southern city. High School football season is in full swing, the teenagers are all at the school. Parents are out with their families cheering on their child playing 3rd string. School has only been in session about two months, daylight savings has not yet become a reality

(Because let's be honest, we're all waiting for that blissful Sunday where we say "Fall Back" and gain an hour of sleep). It is just past nine o'clock and the game is nearly over.

In a small store, located in a strip mall, a group of food service workers are preparing for the late night rush. That time when the crowds disperse from the stadium and head home, their younger children cranky and tired, but ready to eat. Mom and Dad have worked a full week and then carted themselves and the kids out to the stadium to support their oldest child. They begin the drive home realizing what time it is. Mom is tired and has to be up to take kids to soccer practice or dance lessons in the morning. Dad is exhausted from working all week and is hoping to catch up on some sleep before doing yard work that he's been meaning to do for a month before the HOA sprouts horns and begins to hover around the front door of the house talking about fines. So what to do? No one wants to cook and it's already late.

*Ding, Ding, Ding.*

The answer is to order from some restaurant for delivery or pick-up. Whichever is more convenient considering they are already headed home. Typical, Friday night shenanigans. Workers in the food industry know this pattern and prepare for it. The part that gets tricky is when your Arrogant Andy comes into play.

On the side of the co-worker, this is a person who can never be corrected. He or she is always right, and no matter their position, they look down on the other staff. Many times, they proclaim themselves to be studying or awaiting a position in another profession far exceeding the role they currently occupy. This results in their looking down their noses at those who are working in this field full-time. Andy's also are hard to direct from a management standpoint.

A person who believes themselves to be above or better than the position they work, exude this self-confidence in a form of blustery and prickly rudeness. Typically, they insult or degrade not only their coworkers, but customers in certain circumstances. One such person worked on the crew at this small food store on this particular Friday night.

This Arrogant Andy, was a delivery driver who was currently on a leave of absence from his chosen vocation as a therapist. It did not matter that he was forced on his little leave of absence, or that he had been on leave for such an amount of time that he had to seek out other employment in order to pay bills. Oh, no.

This employee was a dyed-in-the-wool narcissist with the arrogance to flaunt it. He called his other coworkers, morons. Constantly belittled the staff by saying they only worked these jobs because they were too stupid to find anything "real". Yet, he was here, in this store, working among them because life had taken a turn.

    To his credit, he did not bow his head in shame for the job he worked. However, his downright dismissive attitude and rude interactions did far more to alienate him from the other staff. Which is what started the issue that was about to swirl through the doors of this quiet little food restaurant. Because our Arrogant Andy coworker was about to meet up with his customer counterpart.

    Now, in the customer field, one defined as an Arrogant Andy, is completely self-absorbed. This is the type of person that believes because they are the customer and their time is important, everything should be done immediately. For the sake of clarification, this small food restaurant, is in fact a pizza place. They have the capability to order online in order to ensure they get their food and pick up their food in a timely manner. Whether one calls in an order or uses an app to order online, many people fail to take into account that it takes time to make an order. Especially in a business where the food is not prepared or made until the order is actively on the screen.

    With this in mind, it should be noted, that in a situation like this, it is not like chain restaurants with a drive-thru. There is no pre-made food that can just be built in thirty seconds. Instead, the dough has to be stretched, sauce and cheese applied and then toppings added before it is run through an oven to ensure it is baked to temperature and safe for consumption. All in all, this can take as little as fifteen minutes, or as long as thirty minutes dependent on the time of day and the number of orders that have also been placed around it.

However, customers that are Arrogant Andy's do not take this into consideration. These are people who believe because they are who they are, the second they finish their order, if they appear at the restaurant the food will already be waiting. It doesn't matter if they just hung up the phone less then two minutes earlier, or hit send on the app as they were pulling into the parking lot. It is assumed that the food they ordered, whether it is per the recipe or with their own exceptions, is ready to be handed over the second it is created. Sadly, that is not reality. Not even with chain restaurants that have drive-thru service. It takes time to prepare an order, more so when there are specific requests that deviate from the company standard.

In this scenario, the above assumption came with an order of six pizzas. As if that were not bad enough, it was accompanies by a slew of sides including three sets of wings, a dessert brownie, a two liter drink and a whole stack of differing dipping cups. The order came through and hit the screen to be made at 9:04 pm. All six pizzas were considered specialties – i.e. - They were specific as to toppings in order to meet a certain brand recipe. Still, as is their prerogative, each one had toppings removed or added to one half of the pizza or the other, which essentially made twelve different pizzas.

    I get it. You are probably wondering, how I can remember such an order all this time later. Allow me to inform you, that in the middle of a rush, such as this, where everyone and their mother orders on a certain day, certain things stick out. Sure, you expect to be busy. Essentially most orders during this time frame, consist of a pizza and perhaps one or two sides. So when in fact you get a large order like this, that no one called in ahead of time – it stands out on your screen because it takes up nearly the whole surface of the display. Worse, when there are a lot of adjustments such as removing a topping from one side, or list of toppings from one side, and adding a lot of different ones, you again, see this one order take up almost the entirety of the screen in the kitchen area.

    True, you are working this job in food service and it is your mission to give the customer what they want, but something this particular takes time. One thing that people forget is that everyone is human. The more you change something, the more likely it is that there will be a mistake, something small that gets overlooked in the sudden push for efficiency and quick service people have come to expect. In an order such as this where you are making twelve different pizzas on six pieces of dough, it is especially challenging and stressful.

Especially when you consider this huge order, that no one called in ahead of time so there would be sufficient preparation, had come in between fifteen other orders at the same time.

There is no going around this. You cannot work on the other smaller orders because of the sheer volume of this one. There is no scrolling past it and making the simple orders beneath, because as one would expect you make the food in the order that it comes into the store. So, now, knowing that more than twenty households are waiting on their dinner, you have to try and accurately make these complicated pizzas as quickly and efficiently as possible so you can make sure everyone who has ordered gets their food in a timely manner.

This particular night, the large order was placed and as we were trying to prepare food, the customer who ordered pulled up outside of the store. The managers, seeing the large volume of food on the order, have gone to the prep area in the kitchen to help prepare the food and get it in the oven faster. The other employees, are manning the phones and front counter in an effort to mitigate service and keep things flowing smoothly while the screen is cleared. The sound of a car horn being laid on heavily sounded outside, but as we were in a strip mall, no one really paid it any mind. Instead, employees were greeting customers in the lobby and checking them out with their orders while we continue to work on the never-ending list of food that was on the screen in the kitchen. Keep in mind, even as we work, new orders are coming in at the bottom of the screen, so we are under the gun to continue working to get everything in as fast as possible.

Now, out Arrogant Andy employee is standing off to the side, letting the others in the store handle the customers while he looks on in disgust. It was clear he had no use for helping the customers, and no intention of doing so. Instead, he stood not even one foot away from the front counter, watching his coworkers speak with the customers while checking them out on the registers and handing over their food. He did this from a position that forced everyone on staff to move past him, back and forth, to grab what they needed for customers, essentially putting him in everyone's way.

The car horn outside continues to blare, several short bursts followed by a long extended one. Clearly, this is intending to get someones attention, yet it does not because of the hustle and bustle inside with a line of customers straggling in to obtain their food. When the constant assault of noise does not work, out Arrogant Andy customer escalates his behavior. So begins the flickering of bright headlights to normal lights in the storefront window. Despite popular belief, this is not an action that one can consider non-aggressive. Instead, its distracting and downright rude. Not only is this person trying to force employees to give them attention when they are not even in the store, they have now chosen to blind all of the staff at the front counter actively helping customers, as well as the staff in the kitchen behind the counter trying to make food. The bright bursts of light throwing glares on the screen where the orders are displayed to be prepared and stopping the general flow of traffic within the restaurant.

If you believe this is where the story ends, you are sadly mistaken. Between the flickering high beams, the now nearly constant blare of the car horn, and the customers in the lobby now complaining that service is slowing down we have begin the whirlwind of adversity.

Employees are now uncomfortable because they cannot see and are stumbling over their words while they squint their eyes to look at the screens on the register to give customers their orders. The kitchen is in chaos because no one can see the screen thanks to the customer impatiently flicking their high beams, which causes production to grind to a halt.

At this point, one of the managers trying to help make food, asks the employee who is not helping customers (That's right! You guessed it, the Arrogant one), to go outside and see if they can help the person trying to get our attention. More in an effort to rectify the problem with serving other customers and the staff, than anything. There is a huff, and a puff, but said employee then begins plodding out the side door to walk around and speak to the customer outside.

Meanwhile, operations within the kitchen and lobby area continue. Recovery is somewhat swift, as the big order before us on screen is starting to be placed in the oven. Cue the opening of the side door as our arrogant employee returns and props against the wall near the delivery door exit. He does not speak so the belief is that the person he talked to was not a customer for our store. There is no offering of information, so the rest of the staff continues to handle the hustle and bustle of the dinner rush.

Finally, the large order is now completely in the oven and the staff rush to clear the other orders on screen and make up the precious time they lost. The following orders are all fairly simple and to the point, making the process an easier one. Until the horn blaring starts once more. When the ruckus commences, the flow of the kitchen has been restored and said manager turns back to the employee who went outside and the following conversation takes place.

*Manager:* "So what did the person outside need?"
*Employee Andy:* "He's here to pick up his order."
*Manager:* "Did they already pay for their order?"
*Employee Andy:* "I don't know."
*Manager:* "What's the name on the order?"
*Employee Andy:* "He didn't say."

Cue annoyed narrowing of eyes by manager. Visibly trying to hold back their exasperation, they shift slowly, turning to look at said employee.

*Manager:* "So what are you doing?"

*Employee Andy:* "Waiting on my next delivery."

*Manager:* "Do you think you could go and ask the customer what the name on their order is while you wait? It would also help to know if they paid yet."

*Employee Andy:* "That's not in my job description."

Silence. That is what accompanies this answer. The random sounds of a kitchen pervade the air. The soft clink of metal touching metal as a pizza peel is used to pull pies out of the four hundred and fifty degree oven. The ring of the phone as customers call to try and place orders, but not one of the staff speak a WORD after this Arrogant Andy pulled out the job description card. Even the customers in the lobby seem to realize that this is a pinnacle moment that they should not be a part of.

*Manager:* "Actually, you are here to help the customers, can you please go and ask them what the name on the order is?"

No sooner is this out of the manager's mouth, than said customer comes in the front door. No matter what had been happening before that, the confrontation with the employee pales in comparison to what is about to take place.

*Customer Andy:* "What in the hell is wrong with you people? Where is my order."

*Manager:* "I do apologize, sir. What was the name on the order?"

***Customer Andy***: "I told that employee that came out, I wanted my food. Where is it? I have more important things to do than wait all night for a damn pizza."

***Manager:*** "Again, I do apologize, sir. What was the name on the order?"

***Customer Andy:*** "Williams. Where is my food? This shouldn't be that hard."

***Manager:*** "One second, sir."

Manager proceeds to walk to the heat rack where orders are waiting. There is no ticket for a Williams order. The manager then goes to the computer at the front counter and logs in. Navigating through the displays to find the customer's name and open it on screen.

***Manager:*** "Yes, sir. I see your order right here. It should be out of the Oven in the next five minutes."

***Customer Andy:*** "What do you mean it will be out in five minutes? Do you know who I am? We've already been waiting for twenty minutes."

Manager looks down at the computer, the time is 9:16pm. The order itself did not come into the store until 9:04pm. So already, they are exaggerating.

One thing to take note of, this customer is already irate. They also are so self-involved anything you say will just exacerbate an already difficult situation. You cannot point out that even the website for the store states that their order will be ready between fifteen and twenty-three minutes. Or that they placed their order at 9:04 so the earliest it will be ready is 9:19pm. You also cannot point out that they made an inordinate number of special requests that required longer prep time so the food took longer to get in to the oven. Instead, you have to tread lightly. The sad part of this, is how much you have to demean yourself to placate their anger.

This particular night, the manager tried to smile and apologize again.

***Manger:*** "I do apologize, your order will be out in just a few moments. I see here you haven't paid. We can handle that now if you'd like."

***Customer Andy:*** "What I would like is my food! You're wasting my time. Do you think you could do this one job right?"

***Manager:*** "Sir, I understand you would like your food. Sadly, we have to make our food in the order they come in. Your order is rather large and we already have it in the oven and will get it to you just as quickly as possible. Would you like to pay now to stop from waiting any longer?"

***Customer Andy***: "What I want is for you to do your job? Do I get a discount because I have to wait? You are taking too long."

***Manager:*** "I do apologize you are having to wait. Sadly, there was a little hiccup in reading the screen that delayed your order, but not one that makes your order so late I can offer you a discount. Would you like a 2 Liter for your trouble?"

***Customer Andy:*** "What I want is a discount since you can't do your job. It's not hard. No wonder you don't work a real job."

***Manager:*** "I understand, sir. Would you like to pay now?"

***Customer Andy:*** "Not until you give me a discount and the 2 Liter."

The manager at this point, is struggling to maintain her composure. This customer has already been excessively rude, condescending, and dismissive. It has been explained that his order was almost ready, yet, he thinks his time is so important that it's being wasted because he is waiting for specific food he ordered. Still, she tried, plastering a smile on her face as she responded in kind.

***Manager:*** "Well, sir I can't give you any bigger discount then the one you already got with your coupon online. Again, I apologize for any wait, but your food is coming out of the oven now. Would you like a Coke, Diet Coke, Sprite or Orange Soda?"

***Customer Andy:*** "Coke. Finally doing something to make me happy. I want your corporate number to complain about the atrocious service. Enjoy this job while you have it. My food should have been ready once I hit send."

As the Manager was getting his 2 liter, you could see the facade crack. For a moment, there was a debate as to what would happen. Then she turned around and moved to the counter, placing the 2 Liter in front of the customer while he smirked down on her.

***Manager:*** "Well, sir. I do apologize, but there is no way to have an order that specific ready as soon as you hit send. In order to be sure you get the exact food you ask for, we make your food fresh to order. Which is a good thing too when you want to add or delete whole toppings from part of the pizza to make exactly what you want. While I do apologize for the wait, your food will be exactly as you want it, the total on your order is $74.68."

After that, the customer starts muttering loudly. Insulting the staff as idiots who can't work real jobs. Underlining his importance as to working a real job in the real world. Pointedly saying, "no tip" when he gets to the payment screen despite the other people working hard to be sure he gets his food. As soon as his order comes out of the oven, it is boxed carefully, the order checked and double checked to be sure it's accurate, and then handed directly to him with steam pouring out of the boxes.

**Customer Andy:** "I'll be talking to your store manager tomorrow."

**Manager:** "She will be here at 11 am. Thank you and have a nice day."

In this scenario, the Arrogant Andy Employee made the following situation worse. The lack of attention to details for this job, had him dismissing not only the customer but the manager. In so doing, he got the customer even angrier then they already were, no matter how misguided it may have been and he managed to frustrate the manager. This culminated in the manager also having to deal with an irate and irrational customer in the middle of one of the busiest time of the day.

When dealing with an Arrogant Andy employee, you have to be specific in asking them to do anything. Also, these particular employees will hit back with, "That is not in my job description." It is at that point you have to point out the specifics of the job description on the company policy letterhead, which sadly underlines that when in store as a driver, you do what is needed to help the store run efficiently. Not many want to see or understand that. These employees are a specific kind of headache that require micromanagement because when they get answers they do not like or corrections they don't agree with, they act out. You have to stay on top of them for the duration of their time in store.

When dealing with an Arrogant Andy customer, the best you can do is maintain your calm and hope you can deescalate the situation. Sadly, no matter how calm you pretend to be, they will continue their tirade the whole time they are in store. The best you can do is deal with them efficiently and quickly in order to keep them away from your other customers and the store employees. Most times they will contact higher management and continue to try and make waves, but as long as you follow both policy and procedure you will be fine.

As a customer when you encounter either of these personalities, you can easily navigate them. If someone on the staff of a food or retail store seems dismissive, do not assume all the staff have the same attitude. Shift gears, and address the next person you see. Yes, they may be dealing with another customer and you will need to wait a few moments, but nine times out of ten, it will work out better and less frustrating for you.

If you happen to run into the Arrogant Andy customer and they are in your general area, ignore them. Give them a wide berth to bluster and blow. Once they finish their tirade and leave, you will have a clear line to the employees in finishing your own transaction.

# CHAPTER 4
# THE BOTTOM LINE

For everything, there is a bottom line.

Whether it is life, relationships, or business there is an intended bottom line for everything. Retail Customer Service and Food Service are no different.

A lot of people do not understand that there is a limit to what we can do in order to fix issues. There is a line where the cost of fixing a problem outweighs the problem itself. It all boils down to one thing: money.

Money. The root of all evil. And in this case, the cause of many a headache among those who work in customer service in any way, shape, or form whether it is retail or food that you deal in.

That bottom line will always be the cost. For instance, let us reflect on food service for the moment. The pizza shop mentioned in our last chapter. There are several possible avenues that one could utilize in order to alleviate a customer issue.

Workers are human, mistakes happen. No one is infallible, not the most experienced line cook, nor the manager that oversees them. Mistakes will and do happen, sometimes because of a simple mix-up, and other because of a lack of attention to detail, whether it be from a distraction or some other malaise. Either way, as a customer or a worker, you will encounter this moment, where a mistake had to be corrected.

No matter the company you work for, they want you to make the customer happy. It does not matter who may be at fault, you want the person paying for services to feel their experience was worthwhile so that in the future they return to your business. So, the first step in any of these scenarios is to listen to the complaint.

This is not always so easy. People who have been given the wrong food, or item, tend to be more than a little short with the person they first talk to after the incident. In the last several years, there has been an increasing number of customers who are downright hostile with any and everyone who talks to them about their complaint. Most times, people just want to be heard, That is not to say you should let them be verbally abusive to you while they do so. Using phrases like "I do apologize, can you tell me what was wrong with your order/item" or "I am so sorry for the mix-up, can you please tell me what happened" are good ways to begin diffusing the situation.

Once the situation has been explained, most companies give the same guidelines for resolving said complaints. Give the customer what they want and something extra for the inconvenience. This however, is where you have to balance, customer service with the bottom line that the company is paying attention to.

Offering a soda, is relatively easy as an addition, the cost is a flat one because you have paid the vendor to carry said soda, so you are not really losing store money when you offer one in regards to an 'I'm sorry' to the customer. It also cuts the cost in labor because it is not something to prepare, and it doesn't really effect your inventory hard because it is in itself, its own product. However, not everyone wants a soda for the trouble and would prefer a dessert or some type of food alternative. You are already remaking part of their order, so to add a second item with the same amount of time to be prepared is not unreasonable.

The price of said items, can be. When you have to watch your bottom line, the cost of the food you are making as an apology matters. When you can offer a dessert that is made of plain dough which only costs forty cents, or offering a brownie which costs three dollars just to order to have in store, the difference is obvious. Yes, you want to make the customer happy, but you also want to maintain control of your inventory cost. If you are remaking a pizza that in truth will only cost you a dollar and some change to make, you don't want to triple the cost by offering a free item worth more then what you are already replacing.

These holes in your inventory, even if they please the customer, can cost a manager in food service their job. Admittedly, there are some customers who will not take no for an answer, in these cases, you end up swallowing the cost. By no means, should this be an occurrence that happens every single time. It is our job, to make the customer happy, but not to do so by increasing cost exponentially. Walking that line is not easy under the best of circumstances. In recent years, with the COVID outbreak as well as the swelling entitlement of the masses screaming the age old adage, 'the customer is always right' makes this part of the job harder to accomplish in a responsible manner.

This is something a lot of customers do not understand. It is impossible to know exactly what is happening in the minds of customers, but it is the job of the manager in these businesses to alleviate that person's concern. That can be hard to accomplish in a society that touts the phrase above while also raising people to believe they can get something for nothing.

It should be noted, that these store policies about giving the customer what the ordered, plus something extra for the trouble has been noted. People are aware of these rules and now, have begun to take advantage of it whenever and wherever they can. It is why, it is imperative to have someone in a management position that is able to accomplish this without giving in and costing the company more than the original order was worth. There is a sense of fiscal responsibility that it imperative to keeping not only these businesses alive, but the customers coming back.

While it is true, if the order had been made right the first time this would never be a concern. Yet, people are only human and mistakes will happen. Sadly, the abuse of the loophole in Food Service to remake the problem in the order and give people something for free, is one that some individuals have chosen to exploit. For that reason, and that reason alone one must understand the importance of cost.

So, what does that mean when it comes to the bottom line?

In customer service, there are two variables that any manager should be able to control: Labor and Inventory. In food service this is the same. The only difference is in how the inventory is handled. Also, there is a distinct difference in how these situations are handled because in retail stores, the ability to control inventory and loss is far easier.

Nowadays, it is common that even in the smallest of retail stores, anti-theft systems are set up to prevent the loss of electronics or high end items that are in the store. All the way from big name chain stores down to the smallest mom and pop store, there is commonly some form of security measure to prevent the loss of items available to the public. Clothing tags, electronic monitoring systems, video surveillance, and staff that are watching the comings and goings of the customers keep the product in retail stores from being lost through theft or damage.

Food service is a different story.

In any restaurant, there is no metal detector or theft system at the door. While yes, there are people on the floor watching the entrance, there is little chance to steal anything directly off the walls or out of the kitchen. Controlling food cost/product in the food service industry boils down to attention to detail. So when a problem arises with an incorrect order, it is something you have to navigate carefully.

Sadly, because most businesses have adopted or adhered to the customer is always right, it had brought with it a wave of people who learned to abuse that particular belief. These loopholes, have forced many businesses to fold in the last fifteen years. COVID certainly hasn't helped matters, but as I said earlier in this chapter it all comes down to the bottom line.

For these businesses, be they food service or retail, it's about the weight of profit that you make. So, you must understand, that in making something right, in correcting a customers issue, you have to do so responsibly. For the most part, people can understand mistakes happen. However, there will always be those that demand far more than they should acquire. Their belief that because a mistake was made, they are entitled to whatever else they want. This is a falsehood.

One of the hardest thing you will ever encounter working in the service industry is standing your ground in the face of a complaining and abusive customer. As a patron, more often then not, people will not intervene when they see another customer throwing a fit or giving staff in any service business a hard time.

As a whole, we all choose to ignore it in the hopes it will be over soon if we just let it happen. A new age is dawning however, one where retail and food service employees are adhering to the rules and paying more attention to the bottom line, because in the end, their jobs rely on it. A food service worker who gives out three hundred dollars in free food, is more likely to be fired, then one who has a reputation for only remaking the problem parts of the order and replacing it. It is hard, to stand in front of a person who is cursing and yelling, and offer to fix the issue with their order. It is harder still to stand there and deny them a high ticket item they demand as an apology for the mix-up. Nine times out of ten this makes them even more irate.

The reason this is even being outlined here in the chapter on the bottom line is so that the public has more of an understanding about the what and why of things. In the end, just like a person's everyday home life, it is all about cost.

So, remember...

Mistakes happen, and the people in the service industry before you are trying to make it right, but there are limits to what they can do. Everyone has a line, and for these people to keep their jobs they have to walk that line in pleasing the customer and saving their business. If you find yourself with a problem, make it known but don't ask for the moon. You'll find yourself pleasantly surprised by what you can get if you allow them to offer you what's available.

## CHAPTER 5
## <u>CLINGY CASSIE</u>

The Clingy Cassie is a rare occurrence.

Sadly, when it happens it is not something you can avoid easily, no matter how much you may want to. Despite the moniker, not all Clingy Cassie's are in fact, female. Some are male, but the idea of what they do and how they operate is the same. For the purpose of our tales in the service industry, having one key descriptor is better then trying to be specific to all those who share a certain trait.

A Clingy Cassie is a hard personality to deal with. At first they seem benign enough, they exist on the fringe of your interaction with customers. They are mentioned in passing while you take an order, or when someone is at checkout mentioning that they are buying a certain object for their significant other. It is only after this transaction that you encounter the Clingy Cassie in full form.

This is never a simple experience. It is always something akin to going into battle in the Old World, where dragons fire singes your flesh and swords pierce the chink in your once perfect armor. No matter the place or business, when you encounter the Clingy Cassie, you will not escape unsinged. These satellites to the person you directly had contact with, appear from their shadow and become one of the worst experiences of your life. Again, we will use an incident from the food service industry to highlight one such encounter.

Enter, Jane. Jane is a soft spoken woman who enters the lobby of a pizza restaurant on a quiet, Thursday afternoon. It is midday, about three o'clock, with very little taking place other then preparation for the night shift dinner rush. She is a middle aged woman, dressed in shorts and shirt. Her hair is tied back and she moves into the store with an almost timid demeanor. She is pleasant, greets the staff and asks if she can place an order.

As one would expect, she is greeted and told that of course she can place the order. It should be easy enough to get it made for her quickly. The order itself is simple, two pizzas. One of those pizzas is the specialty for an all meat special recipe, the other is a thin crust pepperoni and mushroom. As unassuming as this order would seem to be, it was only the beginning of a cluster fuck of massive proportions.

The average make time for the order was about two minutes. Which means that two minutes after the person at the computer hit 'send' both of those pizzas were in the oven. On average, the cook time for any order was eight minutes, so when you factor that in as well, for the full course of the order you were waiting maybe ten minutes. In that time, Jane left the store to venture to one of the shops nearby, leaving those in the pizza place to their work.

Time passed as it will, other orders came in and were made to be picked up or sent out. The staff moving around to the hustle and bustle of the mid-day shift. It is here that you find what is close to the twilight hour for a restaurant. That space of time between morning shift, where part of the workers leave and the time when all of your crew for night shift will begin trickling in the door. This time of day is very finite. All it takes is one wrong order when you have a minimum number of staff to disrupt the whole of service that you have been building all morning. Considering service number are what these restaurant companies thrive on, it is not truly something you can afford to lose based on one hour.

Before you ask, there is no scheduling more people to work this time. Essentially you do not have the sales to cover the extra pay and since labor is part of your bottom line you have to adhere to company allowance. In the labor tools set forth by the company, you can only schedule X amount of people based on sales, and if you try to schedule over, well…let's just say it doesn't end well. So, back to Jane.

She has ventured off to another establishment, and business has carried on. Her order comes out of the oven where it goes through the final process of preparation and presentation for the customer. Once the pizza is cut and boxed it is placed on a shelf warmer until the customer arrives to pick it up. Pretty simple process and one that ensures the customers food does not get cold.

Yet, when dealing with a Clingy Cassie, you can do everything right but still this will turn in to a confrontation of epic proportion.

Jane had not returned, so the staff continued to do what was needed to prepare for the night shift. Sides are prepared, tables stocked with the different accouterment that would be needed. Delivery bags cleaned and wiped down and since we were in the middle of the COVID protocols, wiping down the lobby, counters, and doors with sanitizer. What should have been a simple transition soon became a nightmare as the bell over the door sounded.

As was expected, we greeted the person who entered only to see Jane walk in to the lobby with someone at her side. This was not a person that we saw with her when she first arrived to order. However, a smile was offered, before the following occurred:

**Manager:** "Welcome back! We have your order waiting for you."
**Jane:** "Thank you."
**Manager:** "Not a problem." Grabs the boxes off the warmer and moves to the counter, setting them down in front of the customer. "Was there anything else I could get for you?"
**Jane:** "Do you have any of those cheese and pepper packets?"

Here is where things began to get a bit dicey.

***Manager:*** "I do apologize, due to COVID we have stopped carrying the paper packets. We do however have shakers available for purchase. They are a dollar twenty-five each and we have them available for both Parmesan Cheese and Red Peppers."

From here out we will refer to Clingy Cassie as CC, especially when one considered this one is Jane's male significant other.

***CC:*** "Are you kidding me? You want to make us pay for cheese and peppers? They were free before."

***Manager:*** "Again, I do apologize, but these were changes made..."

***CC:*** "I don't care what changes you made, give us the cheese and peppers. Tell them, babe."

***Jane:*** "Well, they aren't free. We can just use some at home."

***CC:*** "No, they always gave us this stuff before. Make them give us our stuff."

***Manager:*** "Again, I apologize, but there will be a charge."

***CC:*** "Are you stupid? We said we wanted the cheese and peppers."

***Manager:*** "I understand that, but you will have to pay for them."

***Jane:*** "We have those at home, it's not a big deal."

***CC:*** *Glaring at Jane.* "Why won't you get me what I asked for? Make them give us their stuff we always get."

***Jane:*** *Taking out her wallet.* "Alright."

**CC:** *Knocks wallet out of Jane's hand.* "NO! We aren't paying. Make them treat us like they should. It's their job to give us our stuff."

**Jane:** *Looking embarrassed and apologetic.* "We have to pay for the peppers and cheese. She is doing her job."

**CC:** "We're never coming back here again."

**Manager:** "Again, I do apologize. Have a nice evening."

**CC:** *Standing as close to Jane as possible, using her as a semi-shield between himself and the staff.* "Can we get some napkins, at least?"

**Manager:** "Again, I do apologize, but since the napkins are not individually wrapped they are not considered safe with the spread of COVID. Until the lock-down and protocols clear we will not have any to offer."

**CC:** "Are you fucking serious right now? You don't even have napkins?"

**Manager:** "Again, sir I..."

**CC:** "What is your name?"

**Manager:** "My name is Hennessy."

**CC:** "Well, Hennessy, you're just being cheap. I'm reporting you to your company and we will see if you have a job tomorrow. Stop lying to me and give me my napkins and stuff, now."

There was no way to give this man napkins because of the COVID standards at that time. After this display, there was certainly no way that he would be receiving a free or comped shaker bottle of spices. Instead, he kept himself plastered to Jane's back as he hurled insults and began yelling louder hoping to change what had already been stated to him.

***Manager:*** "Again, I do apologize. The napkins we had, were not individually wrapped and with the spread of COVID..."
***CC:*** "So you're just being cheap. That's bullshit. I'm complaining to your district manager."
***Manager:*** "I understand, sir."
***Jane:*** "I think that is everything." Looking uncomfortable and grabbing the pizza boxes to make her way back towards the door. It was obvious she was embarrassed by the whole ordeal, but what was curious was the fact her counterpart, was trying to get her to stay in the store.

See, the thing about a Clingy Cassie, is they can only bluster and blow when they are attached to someone else. It's as if they can only function in such a capacity if they are doing so with someone else as an audience who will not stop their tirade.

Obviously, in this scenario, despite being in the wrong, it did not stop CC from causing a scene of epic proportion. When dealing with a Clingy Cassie, try and defuse the situation as best you can. Do not yell or shout back. Stick to speaking in a low, even tone of voice and trying to help their counterpart disentangle from the situation. Nine times out of ten, the person they are anchored to is just as embarrassed or frustrated as the people on the receiving end of the tirade.

Be mindful.
Be vigilant.
Read the signs.

Doing all of these things will help you navigate such scenarios a lot easier in the future. There will be times you are unable to fulfill the requests of others whether they are customers or staff, in the service industry. It is all in how you handle these moments that will define who you are.

## CHAPTER 6
## THE DOOM OF DELIVERY

We have become a society that is all about instant gratification. Instead of going out to eat and sitting at a table to enjoy the robust flavors of food, we now press a simple button to have that food delivered to our door. While COVID had a major effect on the service industry, almost requiring people to have supplies delivered to their homes in fear of spreading the Corona virus, the lasting impact of that time remains.

    Sadly, it has also brought to light just how horrible things can be for people who work in the service industry. With this growing sense of instant gratification delivered with absolute perfection, there is also a lack of general well being and gratitude to those who provide those services. In the last two and a half years, the growing demand for such services has increased nearly three-fold while the benefits of providing said services have dwindled to nearly nothing.

    This is not just dealing with food delivery service jobs, but the varying services like UBER, Instacart, and Grocery or Medicine Delivery as well. There have been many arguments on the matter posted across social media platforms. Many people feeling that they should not be required to offer a tip to someone delivering food or items to their home. Some of those arguments have included the opinion that anyone working said job should have gone to school for training or the ability to work a better position in a different field.

The bottom line is, no matter what many may attempt to say on the matter, it is this attitude that will usher in the end of any kind of delivery as we know it. There are many intricacies to delivery driving, no matter the platform, that the general public is not aware of.

To be fair, even being aware of some of those facts will do little to change the stance many of the populace seem to share on the subject. Still, considering this book is meant to expand on the dangers and hazards of customer service for those working in the field and consumers alike, it is only fitting for me to outline these small factoids to give everyone a clear picture of what exactly is taking place. It is only when a person has a full picture of the scenario that they can make an informed decision on any subject. With that in mind, going forward in this chapter, will be the facts about all of these ventures for those that work in delivery services common to food service and general item delivery.

As mentioned in the opening of the book, personal experience has been garnered in the food service industry. However, there were forays into other services before full time employment became an option. While I will expand on those, the first point on delivery is a universal one. The most common thing people have said in their social rantings on tipping for delivery has been, 'Why should I be expected to tip? This is their job.'

While it is a valid point, that this is the job/or choice of employment for some people, there are other factors that consumers choose to forget. Not too long ago, if you needed groceries, there was no choice as to how you would acquire them. There were no delivery services available to the general public. If you needed something as simple as a gallon of milk to serve your child breakfast the next morning, and it was eight o'clock at night, that meant a rushed trip out of the house to the grocery store. So, despite the fact that you had worked all day, picked up the kids from school, attended a parent-teacher conference, carted your child off to their soccer practice, and come home to make dinner and get the kids to bed...your day was not done. Instead, you found yourself putting your bra back on, grabbing a jacket, sliding on the nearest pair of socks only to find out later they were not a matching pair (or color), rushing out the door to jump in the car and try to get to the store before they locked the door to close. The whole time, your mind is racing with the list of things you still have to get done before bed, and the ever growing list or chores you have for tomorrow. Let's not forget, planning out bill payment, filling up the gas tank now that you have driven six extra places in the span of a day, and of course doing the rounds to visit family and friends to keep both the children and adults in your home socially active.

All of this was added stress. It was one more thing in a long list of things that made days seem never ending. Yet, what choice did anyone have? There was no answer to that back then, you either did such things yourself or they did not get done.

The same could be said for other things, like air filters, sound equipment, replacement car parts. Not even two decades ago, these were things that you could not get delivered to your home. Hell, even five years ago, it was hard to get some items anywhere close to your front door.

Times changed, the internet expanded. Companies like Amazon and Ebay made home shopping and delivery more accessible. Yet, still they encountered problems even on the ground. Still do to this day.

Like all things, we could not leave well enough alone. Everything had to go one step further. The idea, that groceries, or simple remedies from the corner drug store could be available at our fingertips, became a demand. We already had restaurant chains picking up delivery service – why couldn't we have the same for everything else?

So began the outcry for more. For ease of access and availability. For a quick buck. For something more than just pizza. Soon enough, we got UBEREATS, Door Dash, and Grubhub. Suddenly, the world was full of possibilities and the shiny new toy we had acquired was perfect. Then reality set in. Wait times became longer, runs were dropped without warning, and finally we ran into a lack of drivers to even continue these services in some areas.

Now there was outrage. HOW DARE THERE BE NO ONE TO DELIVER OUR GOODS?
The answer is simple.
Money.
There is little to no money in delivering food, retail items, or parts to anyone for an extended period of time. Just like the money people made in driving for UBER was not enough to offset the cost of activating oneself for a ride share.

To explain – UBER pays their driver a flat fee for accepting a ride. There is never a guarantee for a tip in this, but a gradual increase in money dependent on the length of the trip. That said, most fares average about six to seven dollars, give or take. That is not to say there are not some cities where that number is actually far less, but on average at the whole of things, this number seems to hold steady. Now, let's say the person working said UBER, works for eight hours. Taking two runs per hour, this is one hundred and twelve dollars in a day.

While that seems passable, one must also consider the cost of operation. Most cars, require gas so you can safely say that you will fill your car at least once. Considering most UBER vehicles are family sedans or larger, the average price of a full tank of gas will be roughly thirty-two dollars if gasoline is sitting at three dollars and twenty cents a gallon. Again, in other areas this will be more expensive, but I digress. So, if you subtract that amount from the one hundred and twelve, that leaves you eighty dollars.

Ah – but we forgot the other costs of operations. Working for UBER means you're an independent contractor, which means you need to set aside part of what you make to pay taxes at the end of the year. So there goes another twenty dollars.

After that, you have to take out money for the comforts that you need for your ride share. Water bottles, hard candies, etc. to offer your passengers in case they find themselves pressed for time and need refreshment. So, you can eliminate another ten dollars there.

Next, you have to consider vehicle maintenance. You have to plan for keeping your car serviced and in working order. Oil changes every three thousand miles, a trip that doubles as you use your car for ride share or delivery work. New tires or tire rotations to maintain your alignment and tread. That is another thirty dollars set aside right there.

Now that you have covered those costs, you have to consider your own needs. Drinks, food, snacks, phone charger for the car, incidentals for the day included – you can subtract another ten dollars. Even if a person was to pack a lunch, there is always something that comes up while one is out and about waiting for ride shares.

In the end, for eight hours of catering to other people, all you have ended up making is a mere ten dollars. That is not enough to pay any sort of bill to maintain a home. At all.

So, there is no money in continuing the work. You can't cover the maintenance for your car to keep it operation and survive. This is why, gratitude is somewhat required. Yet, people think such a convenience is something they are entitled to, that has no real cost associated to it.

Some may guffaw at the above explanation, but it is sadly true. The worst part of this, is that people working in businesses that offer delivery positions are slightly better off, but the truth is, not by much.

In some ways, Door Dash, Grubhub, and UBEREATS, are phenomenal platforms. Yet, they are detrimental to the people contracting under them. The red tape makes it nearly impossible to reliably use such a thing as a primary income source. The cost will rapidly outweigh the rewards. There is no hourly pay, no mileage to be gained. Just a flat fee and whatever tip the customer decides to bestow upon you. Yet, the tips are becoming fewer and far less frequent, which means the runs have no incentive, or pay off. If you are only making a three ninety-nine flat fee to deliver one hundred dollars worth of food to a home fifteen miles away, that trip costs you more than it nets you.

The food service industry offers only a slightly better advantage. These workers get an hourly paycheck for coming in to deliver food to other people. Most of these businesses also offer a mileage rate to compensate for each delivery taken. Most stores offer an average of about twenty-eight to thirty-two cents a mile. While it is not much, it is better than some.

All in all, these drivers face the same issues as people running Door Dash and the like, but with an actual hourly paycheck. This allows them a little extra room for vehicle maintenance and the like, but still it falls short.

Now, the secret. If each delivery tipped even a dollar to these people, whether it was UBER, or some food industry restaurant that offers delivery, these drivers would not be struggling to keep working. They would be making money to cover their costs. True, it may never be a six figure a year job, but it would be something reliable and worth keeping until a better employment opportunity could be found.

Instead, we watch them traipse in and out of the revolving door known as employment. Some, choosing to save themselves the headache of losing their vehicle to too much wear and tear.

Others, to the fact they make less than they need to keep gas in their vehicle, let alone pay bills. People seem to forget that because they wanted something convenient, it still costs others to make such a thing happen.

Delivery is no exception.

If you want to look at the retail side of things, consider the times that a person orders the things required to add on to their house, or new appliances to be installed. There is a fee for the haul of those items to the location for delivery. If they wish to have someone else install those appliances or build that addition, they pay for the service. So why is it that we balk at these costs? Refusal to pay these fees, leads to a lack of employment, and eventually, to a lack of workers to make such services impossible to acquire.

In the end, society as a whole is phasing out service jobs. In both retail and food service we are seeing a marked decline in services. Restaurants are now going to carry-out only and limiting their hours making it harder to enjoy those small luxuries. Retail stores are unable to afford hourly wages because of the demand for delivery from services like Instacart or Uber, so they are installing self-checkouts to control labor costs.

The most ironic part of all of this is that society is becoming more and more annoyed with self-checkout. Asking to be rung up by an employee that no longer exists because that job has been eliminated based on people asking for their groceries and items to be delivered straight to their homes. Self-checkout is literally the culmination of years of society wishing for instantaneous service on demand. Insisting they could do it faster and more conveniently.

When you look at the pattern, this also stands to be a working model for what will happen with food delivery inside the next five years. If the current trend continues, there will be little to no options on having food delivered to ones home from any restaurant or grocery store.

When you weigh the pros and cons of asking for such a service, few people consider it from the perspective of their own wallet. In asking someone to take on the chore of picking up food, or items you need for your home and delivering them to you, there are several aspects that make this beneficial to the consumer.

They will no longer be driving to complete this task, so they will be saving on gas money. There is also the fact they will not be using their time to roam the aisles or lanes in the store in question, instead they will be able to spend their focus on some other task that requires their attention. So now they are saving on time as well. Factor in the lack of action on their own part, there is also less on their plate physically in having to accomplish such a task on their own.

Already with something this simple, the consumer is saving their own time, money, and effort. So if one were to assign a monetary value to such things, like a working wage, or what their time is worth it is safe to assume most would rate that their fee would be costly.

However, when you mention paying people for their time and effort in replacing their presence in doing these tasks, they balk at offering monetary recompense. Instead saying that these individuals should find a better job, or do something more worthwhile if they want to make money. The degradation I have seen some people place on others for working in some form of delivery customer service is appalling. Yet, it continues.

The reformation of the service industry as it steers to a more rigid stance about the customer not always being right, does not stop at the stores themselves. It is also spreading through the workers, the staff. For years, we have tried to preach that society should be more open-minded and kind, yet still we have people that openly deride those in the customer service industry.

Unlike twenty years ago, there is no demand that one stand there and take such abuse. People have been told their feelings matter. That the way they are treated is important. Which leads us to a time like we have now.

Workers who left the customer service industry out of necessity during COVID, are refusing to return. With good reason. They are reluctant to step back into a role that is filled with constant abuse and less gratitude.

However, that is not what the public sees. Instead, they complain about the lack of service that forces them to miss out on these events or experiences they had pre-COVID. People who worked in the customer service industry are content to work other jobs that limit their interaction with the populace. Not that many could blame them. Still, the populace as a whole complains about the lack of workers, how it is ruining their life. Yet, these same individuals are the ones that would refuse to offer a tip to the server who refilled their coffee every five minutes. Or to tip the personal shopper who did their grocery shopping for the month, or the delivery service person who hauled boxes up three flights of stairs for the ease of the customer.

All of these things have perpetuated a new normal. One where instant gratification is no longer possible. Patience is a virtue one must have when dealing with customer service for convenience. That lack of patience is running rampant, causing complaints and more than that, drama. These factors are pushing those people who have held onto these positions to find other employment. Others, are refusing to even consider entering the customer service industry over such experiences. Those that do, rapidly find the exit after finding there is no money in it.

In the end, a lot of these scenarios would go a lot easier if people would weigh things based on their own lives. If it were them, and they had taken the time to do someone else's shopping, drive it twenty miles out of the way, and deliver – what would it be worth? What would cover their costs in doing such?

Something so simple which would be allowing you to see these things from another perspective. So the next time you are dealing with someone in customer service, keep these things in mind, and ask yourself: "With this person's actions, my life is easier, so how much would my time have been worth for the same?"

If things do not change, and do so soon, we will see a sharp decline in delivery services across the board. Once that service is lost to us, there may be no way to get it to recover. As a whole we should consider those things anytime we look at doing something for convenience.

# CHAPTER 7
## ECCENTRIC ERIN

Variety is the spice of life. At least that is what some people say. However, sometimes too much variety can be somewhat off-putting. Which brings us to the next personality you will encounter in navigating the service industry: Eccentric Erin.

Whether this personality comes in the form of a customer or another employee, they are and will forever remain a landmine. While there is no guarantee that the moment of detonation will be detrimental, odds are that nine times out of ten the impact of that explosion will be devastating in some form or fashion. From time to time, these moments where these personalities ignite can be humorous and amusing.

There is nothing to say that Eccentric Erin's are horrible on the whole. Quite the opposite, these personalities can be entertaining. It should also be mentioned that while it can be difficult navigating the waters of interaction with an eccentric, there will never be a dull moment. Most individuals with this type of personality are hard to predict. One moment they can be completely mellow and introverted and in the next they be completely unhinged dependent on the subject at hand. Such an experience is bracing, but manageable.

The thing about the rants of an eccentric, is that you have a hard time keeping a straight face. For the most part, these individuals are just different. Their priorities and the things they lose it over are something small that seem inconsequential to the grand scheme of things. Yet, you cannot help but to find a small bit of amusement at the sheer display of epic proportion over something so small.

The rant of someone labeled as Eccentric Erin, will be a lot of bluster and blow with no real damage. That is not to say it will not cause chaos, far from it. There will be a plethora of chaos to accompany said display. It could be likened to the temper tantrums of a toddler.

If said tantrum comes from a customer, it will be difficult to navigate the situation. Most experiences that have been witnessed, is a situation where the person's hands are tied by policy and the eccentric personality is battling 'the man'. As hilarious as this may seem, sometimes it is extremely difficult to put oneself in a situation where you have to say 'no'. However, when working in customer service, that choice is not always your own. It is the one job where everyone else in the outside world will choose your actions for you.

To understand just what you are dealing with, it is important to understand that the world of the Eccentric is not like the reality the rest of us know. Most individuals that carry this label are the dreamers, the artists, the people that live on the fringe of the real world but experience it differently. This world needs dreamers such as this, but it does not make them any easier to deal with. In most cases, it makes things more difficult.

    The universe at large is different for them. They see things in a different spectrum. Time moves differently for them and the priority list can be more then a little skewed away from what others would consider acceptable. While it can be argued that these traits make individuals more unique, that certain twist to their personality that differs from the norm makes them harder to interact with. Deescalation in these cases is somewhat more difficult, because their world view is so different from others. Part of being a good worker in Customer Service is to put yourself in the customer's shoes in order to try and fix their issue.

    That particular ability can be a little more difficult than normal with an Eccentric Erin. Honestly, it can be downright debilitating when one of these personalities is an employee as well. The issue stems from the way they view the world differently. It is generally difficult under any circumstance to try and view the world from the perspective of another person. With eccentric personalities, that aspect of whimsy that makes them one of the artists and the dreamers, fixates on an object , item, or event that is seemingly unimportant in the general flow of everyday life for other people. That is the hardest part of deescalation with an eccentric personality, is pinpointing just what it is that has them so upset to begin with.

Make no mistake, these personalities are essential to society as a whole, but they can be slightly difficult to manage. Whether they are a customer or an employee, these situations will be dicey. They are already upset, and a misstep in either direction can make the problem explode into something exceptionally worse. The term, kid gloves definitely applies.

Realistically, ninety percent of the interactions one has with people with an eccentric personality is enjoyable. On the normal day in general circumstances, they are bubbly and bright, filled with laughter or small anecdotes to make you chuckle to yourself. Their world view is a brilliant one, that forces you to look outside the normal box that you perceive the world in.

Eccentric personalities are the friends or customers you have that look up at the sky and say, 'Hey, that cloud looks like a dinosaur' or 'That plane right there, looks like a small ant sailing through the air towards an ant hill'. They see through a lens that most of us shed when we are children. The world is a giant adventure that they wish to explore and everything is full of new and wonderful opportunities. At least, until there is a hiccup and something goes wrong.

The moment that such an event takes place, it grinds their whole world to a halt. That normally bubbly personality become a roiling cauldron of rage and anger. That anger, usually comes in the form of yelling or seemingly childish antics. There can be crying and temper tantrums, nothing like the violent ones seen on social media. Mostly, with eccentric personalities, once you find the root of the problem and correct it, the bluster and blow quiets down. The rage recedes and the only thing left is a burned out shell of the bright light that had been there before.

However, as both employees and customers, these personalities can be some of the most loyal and trustworthy people you will ever come across. When you spend the time to fix their issue or help them through these moments of turmoil – they do show a propensity for returning to help or as a customer, buy things when you are present for them. It is a balance system of risk versus reward.

From the standpoint of a worker in customer service, whether it is food or retail, handling customer concerns for an eccentric personality can be very trying. The reward however is that much sweeter. For example, an eccentric customer who orders a food with a lot of specifications that are out of the ordinary places an order. Their food is made and given to them but there is a mistake. The minute that mistake is found the customer will explode. They will bring you the food and yell that it's not what they asked for. That they don't understand what the problem is with getting their order correctly.

The way in which you handle this situation is key. Yes, to you it might not be earth-shaking that someone forgot to put a black olive on that sandwich or pizza. To them, it is a distinct discourse in their day. Without that black olive, that sandwich or item is not going to be as good as it could be. It's not what they want or expect so it's going to be absolutely horrible. There would be some who would ignore the rant, and dismiss the customer after promising to fix the problem with a different sandwich. While yes, this is acceptable, it will do nothing to soothe the temper and upheaval for the eccentric personality before you.

Same scenario, but instead of just offering a remake and forgetting the problem, you instead apologize. Engage with the customer and ask them for the specifics of what they want in their order. At that moment, when you ask for such a thing and they feel like you really do want to make them what they wanted, they will open up and start a long winded explanation. As tempting as it will be, do not tune them out. Actually listen. These eccentric personalities are also creatures of habit, so if you hear them out, you will learn exactly how to avoid such problems in the future. Taking such an interest, will also make them feel like they are that important and they will be returning to you time and again for service.

Now, in retail it will be a slightly different scenario. The problem could be not having a specific brand of item, or a certain color. You can however, underline that you can fix the issue, but it may be a couple of days as you have to wait for deliveries. In the end, it will be the effort you put in to THEM and in fixing THEIR problem, that solidifies their future patronage.

With eccentric employees, it is an altogether different situation. In warning, these people are the ones that are a catalyst among the whole of the staff. People with eccentric personalities tend to be a lightning rod among crew members. They will fall into one of two categories among staff: they will be absolutely loved or they will be the person on staff no one seems to understand or get along with. Both scenarios come with their own problems.

For the personality that is accepted by the staff and earns their support, they can become some of the things of nightmares. These employees, while great for morale, can also shake at the foundations of the store. They influence the mood of others without even realizing they are doing it. Sadly, that influence can set the tone for the whole of the evening. When they are upset, the world is upset. With that, an angry staff is a frustrated staff and more prone to make mistakes. Another pitfall, resides in the actions of the management. If the eccentric personality makes a mistake, one they have been warned about before, and a manager tries to correct them – it polarizes the staff against the management. The favor that the eccentric personality has cultivated among their peers, also brings those peers forward to try and protect that person when they are being corrected. Which can cause for several tense and often uncomfortable moments.

On the other side of the spectrum, the eccentric personality that has alienated the staff can be disruptive to a heightened degree. These persons, knowing they are the odd one out, then seek to become as disruptive as possible in order to find someone, anyone to be on their side and seeing things their way. Such is not realistic, but that is not the way they see things. Instead, they search for an ally among the staff, a chink in the armor if you will. They seek someone who will side with them on any and everything on the job site in order to be sure they are not alone.

Sadly, this is disruptive and anyone in a position of management will find themselves constantly having to pull this person aside. There will be conversations about disruptiveness in the workplace. About the rest of the staff feeling uncomfortable. Then as the issues progress, there will be conversations about a lack of reliability on that person's part. It is not an enviable position to be in. Sadly, it will also make you the subject of that particular person's ire. They will seek to be verbally antagonistic whenever they get the chance. It will not matter if it is another manager or employee, their need to shift the narrative, to make the world see things the way they do, makes it almost imperative that they cause such disruptions to get others to see what they do.

In the end, when dealing with such a personality, again the key is to hear them out. While you may not necessarily agree with them and they might be doing things completely outside of the acceptable practices of your business, pulling them aside and listening to their perspective will get you far. In the process, it allows you to understand their way of thinking and then calmly explain the whys and whatnot's of the workplace. True, this approach will not always work. When it does, however, you will end up with an employee that is willing to walk through fire to learn what to do correctly because you took the time to listen and address their point of view. While you may have to correct it in some aspects – the way in which you handle it can either improve the situation or make things worse on the whole.

In closing, for eccentric personalities, there is a modicum of things to be prepared for. Enjoy their bubbly side, their view of the world. Take the good along with the bad. Remember, they just want to be heard, to have someone see the world as they do. While you may not be able to do that, you can listen and forge a bridge where they will be the best parts of your day as either a customer or an employee. Take their issues as seriously as you can and let them tell you what they want or need. I promise, the moment you show such an interest in what they are actually wanting or looking for, you will find the situation far easier to navigate.

## CHAPTER 8
## FORGETFUL FRANKIE

We have all experienced a moment of forgetfulness. Whether it's leaving our keys in the car, forgetting our cell phone at the house on the charger, or leaving our wallet in our other outfit. We are human, and sometimes we just forget the little things because of a time crunch or even a particular difficulty that is resting on our minds. It happens. However, sometimes it is a little more than something so simple. Which brings us to our next personality.

Forgetful Frankie.

I get it, you believe this can't actually be a personality type. After all, everyone forgets stuff once in a while.

Let me assure you, this is a personality. It exceeds leaving behind small physical objects at home when you may need them otherwise. In truth, this amount of forgetfulness is beyond the pale.

We will speak of this personality from both sides of the customer service experience. To begin, we will be outlining the customer side of things. Working in customer service is already a difficult task, but when confronted with a Forgetful Frankie it becomes a little more than frustrating. Something that one must consider, is customer service is all about fine details. The smallest things have to be accounted for in the long run. Running a register is not just running a register. It is a string of events meant to enhance the customer experience. You greet the customer, ask if they found everything alright. From the moment they walk up you try and engage with them so they know that your attention is solely theirs.

With a Forgetful Frankie this is just the beginning of the struggle. There is nothing to prepare you for a personality like this one. Well, there is but it isn't as helpful as you might think it is. Dealing with a Forgetful Frankie is much like dealing with a toddler hyped up on sugar. You will never lead the conversation, there will never be an explanation for some of the questions, but there will be a delay in finishing whatever task you are doing.

This is not meant maliciously. Not at all. It is merely a statement of fact that sometimes when dealing with a person who has a tendency to be described as a little ditzy, the encounter will not be an easy one. It never is. When you are checking anyone out that has this personality, there will inevitably come a question that when you answer will elongate the scenario. It could seem innocuous at first, but soon enough you will see how that one question rolls downhill into a series of questions that you were not prepared for.

These conversations, when they happen, require patience. It is not the easiest of tasks, and from time to time you will feel the urge to roll your eyes in the back of your head. As much as that urge overcomes you, it is best to keep yourself as focused on the conversation as possible, because the minute you show this frustration to a Forgetful Frankie, they will shift gears and start down another path that is completely divergent from your goal of helping to get them situated and on their way home. If you do so, the encounter will last far longer than you are prepared for.

So, when the question arises, your best bet is to answer in succinct sentences. This conversation usually begins with the customer asking something along the lines of, 'Do you carry this particular item?' Now, in retail, you would tell them if you did carry that item and where exactly it would be located. From there, one of two things happen. They send whoever has accompanied them to the store to go and find said object, or they go themselves and say that they will be right back. Either situation has its own complications, but navigating through them can be fairly painless. This one question begins a spiral effect, because once you have answered, they inevitably ask, 'So if you have that item, where would I find this other item to go with it?' It would be nice to say that this is not common, but it is far more common then you realize.

With a Forgetful Frankie, that one answer to their question begins a new thought process. Now that they know they can acquire said item, they are thinking of the other accompanying items around it. Whether they are ingredients, or utensils, or something as simple as serving ware and aluminum foil. Often times with these individuals, one thing usually triggers a rapid roll of follow-up thoughts that are hard to contain.

    In food service, this same scenario is a little more tricky. The reason for this, is that it helps in adding to your sales by doing something called up-selling. However, it has a disadvantage in the fact that it requires anyone who is helping them to run through the items on the menu. These orders will be more complicated and require a lot of attention. The specific items will be added to and have normal items removed from them, and when you think that it is complete, you will start on another item and they will say, 'Oh, I forgot, can I add this to this item from before?' Then comes the end. When you get to this part, a normal script for any food industry store is to ask if they would like to add something to the order. Whether it's sauces or a dessert, that question can open up a litany of new items that a Forgetful Frankie had otherwise forgotten about. Then they will ask if you have certain things available and the list of questions will begin again. It is trying to remain patient for such a thing, but the best thing you can do is to calmly run through the list with them. Especially in food service, where the objective is to up your sales as much as possible.

However, under the best of circumstances deal with a Forgetful Frankie is difficult. When something goes wrong with their orders, the interaction becomes something a bit more complex then one would expect. What makes this difficult, is determining whether or not the mistake was from misunderstanding what the person wanted on their order, or if they forgot to add it in the first place. Which you will question when you go to correct the problem and ring up the remake and it ends up getting different toppings or items added to the order.

These situations are more common then you might think. On some days, anyone can become a Forgetful Frankie because of whatever events are taking place. It is important to remember, that on any day where you have a ton to do, it is easy to get overwhelmed and when that happens you may look for something to make the day go a little more smoothly. To take something off your plate to try and hurry things along. So you might be the person standing at the counter, who is placing an order, but forgets to add onions, or peppers, or sardines to an order. You could be the shopper that asks about where to find a particular item in the store, and then remember you need something altogether different. So, remember that when you are dealing with anyone who seems like a Forgetful Frankie. Especially one in the scenario we are now moving on to, the co-worker.

While a Forgetful Frankie customer may seem trying, it is nowhere near as frustrating as a co-worker that falls into this category. If there were some sort of platitude to be offered for this scenario, it would be mentioned here, but the sad truth is, there is not one that fits. While yes, we can all have a single day where we adopt the Forgetful Frankie persona, there are some individuals who live that life everyday.

Eventually, there is one of these individuals hired on every staff in customer service. Food service, retail, the actual sub-class doesn't truly matter. The only thing that can be guaranteed, is that eventually this is a trait you will deal with every single day.

At first, it will be amusing. A new worker, trying to learn new standards and operating procedures, there is no way to actively hold that much new knowledge and remember it every single time. However, once the training is done, once the person have proven to be able to navigate the job at least somewhat skillfully, it becomes more than a little frustrating to have to remind a person again and again about certain details.

You will find yourself having to underline or remind these individuals about particular details that you would think are self-explanatory. There is no finite or definitive way to get a person comfortable with their job. Every person is different in regards to how they learn or process information given to them in order to perform in their given position. Yet, with a Forgetful Frankie all of those varying methods or styles will not help you in tempering their forgetful nature. For these few, there is nothing to do but calmly wade through the troubles you will encounter with them.

Make no mistake, they will be sweet individuals. Most people with a forgetful personality, are not bothered by the same things a majority of people find frustrating. Their ability to listen to instruction and then immediately forget and let go makes them unique in such regard. They do not sweat the small stuff that most people are hyper-vigilant about. That is not to say that things with these individuals are easy. There will be times when their lack of attention to such details because they seemingly forgot will be tiresome. In food service it will also make things more difficult, especially if or when they work through a dinner rush.

The time that it takes to complete orders, or get customers the service they wish for will increase exponentially. While it is inevitable that something will go wrong because we're all human and mistakes are made - with a Forgetful Frankie the sheer amount of incidents from missing small details will increase. These small steps that are forgotten can be something as simple as hitting the 'finish' button for an order, so it never gets put in the system, or as mind-numbing as having most of an order ready for distribution to find out that one of the items is missing an ingredient or something the customer has asked for.

    While the personality of a Forgetful Frankie can be amusing, and downright fun in most circumstances, in high pressure work situations it is less than ideal. That is, of course, working under the assumption that the worker in question made it to their shift without difficulties from their particular quirks. It is not uncommon for a Forgetful Frankie to arrive for their shift lacking the necessary tools for their job.

    No matter the business you work in, be it customer service or a high end office, there are certain tools required to perform your duties. People that share this personality, have a tendency to come to work unprepared. In such times, it falls on management and other staff to make exceptions in order to allow that person to function at work. While this could be something as simple as finding them a pen and paper, or sending them back home to retrieve forgotten items, it has a definite affect on the work environment itself. The time that it takes to make these accommodations leaves you short one staff member at the very least. If management or another co-worker need to be present in re-outfitting the employee, then you are now short two people. No matter the work environment or job, being short two people at any given moment, monumentally increases the workload on the rest of the staff.

Admittedly, while a Forgetful Frankie may be amusing to interact with in part, scenarios where their forgetfulness infects the work environment as a whole are not ideal. In some cases, it fosters a resentment with their co-workers, or makes it abundantly clear that they should not be working in the position they hold. If it is the latter, then there is of course, the task of dismissal which is difficult even under the best of circumstances. When it is someone whom you like or are amused by, letting them go from your staff is difficult. Especially when you consider the job market today.

Still, you must weigh the benefit of their presence against the disruptiveness that it brings. It is hard to justify keeping someone employed who makes constant mistakes. Who arrives for their shift lacking the basic tools needed to perform their job. These basic tools can range from a writing implement to a part of their uniform. Without either of these things the whole of their progress on shift will grind to a halt until you make an exception to get them the tools the forgot or lack so that they can function. That is also not addressing having to stop whatever you are doing to correct their actions when they miss a step or forget some key point in executing their tasks.

If you spend a majority of your time correcting their mistakes or having to help them complete the tasks they are given, you are unable to perform your own duties. In the end, the cost of having two people to do the same task that could be accomplished by one, will weigh out. Especially in a society that embraces capitalism as its form of business model.

In the end, a Forgetful Frankie can be detrimental to the long term goals of your business, especially in the customer service industry. People take comfort in being acknowledged, remembered and recognized. Something that this particular industry thrives on. So a Forgetful Frankie is not likely to make it far, no matter how charming their personality. That is not to say you do not have options, you have several. There is always a hope that you can implement or foster behaviors that will make a difference and perhaps improve certain aspects of their forgetfulness to be a non-issue.

It will not be an easy thing to accomplish, but there are things you can do in order to help a Forgetful Frankie in the workplace. When dealing with one of these personalities, do your best to foster a support system that will make it hard for them to forget their tasks or how to complete them. Sometimes mnemonics can work in helping them to remember step-by-step guides in dealing with tasks they will do repetitively. To offset forgetfulness with work tools, most businesses, have supplies that will allow you to negate that to some degree. You can however, make extra of any of those tools available so that a day of forgetfulness is a non-issue. Sometimes, the tools necessary are out of your hands, such as a workers personal cell phone, laptop, or other such objects. While there is little that can be done from anyone else's perspective, one can encourage a person with a forgetful personality to set alarms or the like as reminders to make such things a non-issue. In extreme circumstances, knowing that these things may happen, the manager in charge working on scheduling can put the Forgetful Frankie on the schedule to come in half an hour early or before they are really needed. Doing so, allows for a brief window where the person can return home to retrieve their items for work and be back before they are really needed.

    There is hope on all sides for people that have a Forgetful Frankie personality. As mentioned earlier, their perspective of life is one that is easy going and allows them to get along with everyone, customer or employee. Take advantage of that and do what you can to nurture them in the environment in which you come in contact with them.

# CHAPTER 9
# THE GABBER

There is no cute name or moniker for this one. Honestly, this particular personality will just be attacked head on.

    Whether it be at work or home, some particular personalities are unavoidable. The Gabber is one that exists in every environment. Family, Friends, Acquaintances, Frenemies, Co-workers: among every group there is one individual that lacks the ability to just shut the hell up. Admittedly, there are some cases where there is a reason for someone that talks all the time. Personally, having experience with high functioning Autism and Asperger's, people afflicted by these conditions have no choice in their personality quirks or traits.

    However...

    This universe has been kind enough to gift us with individuals that lack the common decency to realize there are limits. The Gabber is one of these people. This is a person, who despite social queues or pointed warnings about the subject matters upon which they choose to speak, continue onward.

    Admittedly, there is always a time when we as people get excited. We wish to share that excitement with the world around us. These events are one off and uncommon to say the least. With a person who is a gabber, these events are not once in a blue moon, but **every...single...day**.

Sadly, in the case of such a personality, there incessant talking is not on subjects of interest. Worse, nine times out of ten, they are spewing nothing more than supposition and gossip. There is no legitimacy to their claims, just a need to speak to hear themselves talk. Worse, in the work environment, whether they are an employee or customer – the level of sheer annoyance that they inspire with others is a hurdle that is dangerously hard to overcome.

The Gabber has the ability to set anyone's teeth on edge. The minute they draw a breath and it is understood they are about to launch into some long-winded story or diatribe, a person is already seeking to find something to distract them. While this would seem to be the better solution, it comes with inherent risks. If the person in question is an employee or co-worker, tuning them out could cause a complete break down in communication among the whole staff. Especially if you miss some question that is asked of you or your attention is so divided that you miss a detail on the task you are performing. Such a thing can cause complete chaos among the workplace.

Now if said Gabber is a customer, tuning them out could bring an incident down on your head that makes it difficult to remember why you are trying to keep a job in the first place.

The Gabber does not take kindly to being dismissed. At the risk of sounding like an arm chair psychiatrist, one thing to be noted is that individuals with this personality are typically narcissists. The belief for them is that the world as a whole, revolves around them and what they have to say. Whatever is happening to them, or that they speak of happening to them, is what can be considered the top priority above all things. In customer service, the job is to put the customer first. With a person like The Gabber, your patience will wear thin quickly.

To put such in perspective, consider a family reunion or get together. Everyone has encountered this situation before. That one family member who appears at the function and the whole of the room seems to go silent and still. The arrival of this individual causes most conversations to still, with no one willing to continue speaking about whatever had been so important the moment before. There is a distinct lack of interest in sharing information with the newly arrived family member. Instead, the majority of the room turns to nonsensical topics like weather or football. However, this does not stop the new arrival family member from jumping into one or several conversations beginning their diatribe with something along the lines of 'did you hear about what happened with such and such?' So begins, the gossip. They will outright start spreading half-truths about other family members present, beginning some drama that we run home to complain about.

The Gabber is an instigator. There are no ifs, ands, or buts to it. So dealing with one that is a customer is like walking through the lava field of an active volcano. One misstep, and you will get severely burned. In dealing with a customer that you could deem 'The Gabber' they will always have something to say. Always. Whether it is about someone who works in the same business as you, or about the company that produces one of the products they are trying to procure. There seems to be a limitless amount of information from this individual. Make no mistake, nine times out of ten they are merely talking out of their ass, but the sad fact of the matter is, you can do nothing to stop them.

Worse, when you are at work, and are bound to answer their questions and interact with them, it becomes the golden opportunity. While these individuals spend most of their time speaking out to garner attention, good or bad – anyone that works in the customer service industry becomes their captive audience. It does not matter if you are unaware of who their mother's sister's cousin's husband is. The Gabber will happily begin informing you of the latest 'trouble' beset upon the couple or person in question. Worse, you have to give them your attention and your time. Failure to do so, will result in one of the most uncomfortable confrontations that people in the service industry try to avoid.

Be aware, The Gabber is not to be taken lightly. Be they a customer, or an employee, these individuals are destructive to the world around them. Dealing with anyone who could be considered A Gabber, will not be easy. Often times, they are selfish individuals who pride themselves on being the center of attention and the do all, know all of their environment. Any attempt to illuminate that fact, or push them aside as an afterthought, will be met with a stunningly exaggerated and sometimes mind-numbing response. These moments with The Gabber are crucial, especially if they are trying to underline some point in dealing with another individual in your store or a company in direct competition with your own. They have to be the person in the know and explaining to you why things are the way they are.

These moments will be difficult to say the least. As such, when you encounter a person with The Gabber personality, you have to balance your personal feelings apart from your eventual goal. The situation, whether you are another customer in a store, a customer service worker at a register dealing with The Gabber, or a fellow employee, is one you will have to navigate carefully. The best way to do so, no matter the above scenario you are facing, will be exactly the same.

In dealing with one of these individuals, be polite. This is the number one rule in this scenario. As long as you greet them civilly and begin the conversation, you have a chance to guide the conversation and move the interaction along more quickly. Admittedly, this will not always work and you will have to follow the conversation to where they lead. However, if you are able to lead the conversation, the minute they veer off into any sort of gossip, you can smile politely and respond with short but non-committal answers.

Saying phrases like, "I did not know that' or 'No, I was not aware, I will have to look into that', will end the subject at hand one way or another. Whether they feel justified in the sharing of the information they just offered, or as if they have won some unknown prestige for being informed, they have a tendency to back off after you have given them some kind of confirmation that they have given you up to date information. No, this is not the most honest means of dealing with such an occurrence, but it is effective.

Next, you can shift the tone of the conversation by asking about the items they are purchasing. Or in some cases, asking where specifically they have found those items. In food service, you replace these questions with specifics about their order. Would they like an additional flavoring or ingredient on their order? If they ordered something with dipping cups available, would they care to purchase extras? There are always questions to ask, and if you do so in a manor that alludes to them, and what they like and prefer, it can rapidly change the gossiping path of the conversation.

During the last part of the interaction, you can nod your head when they mention something. Soon after, you smile and thank them for their time and give them the total of their bill. If they start to balk, you can swiftly interject with a, 'would you like to pay with cash or card today?' Most often this is a flag of the end of the transaction and the conversation. Sometimes, it does not work as a deterrent, but in most scenarios, especially in the economic climate with items costing more, it is effective.

Finally, and for the love of all that is holy, do not forget this part.

Make sure you tell the person, 'Thank you.' This can also be paired with, 'Have a wonderful day.' The Gabber loves being the center of attention, and despite the fact that you are asked to always be polite with customers and thank them for their patronage, putting the effort into your parting words with these particular individuals will make them all the happier if they feel they have left you hanging. Willing for more the next time, or content in the knowledge they have shared with you that day.

Sadly, for the rest of us, dealing with The Gabber as another shopper or bystander is really painful. You're annoyed with their need to be the center of attention and with making your task in shopping or interacting take twice as long because they will not move along. There are ways to proceed, though most can be perceived as rude. In some cases, these actions act as a lightning bolt for an individual who is a Gabber and causes them to move along. In others, it turns their ire in your direction. So, use discretion in what you choose to do and can handle on that particular day.

    The ways of dealing with the Gabber in these social situations is to insert yourself to derail them. In the case of general public scenarios when The Gabber has finished their transaction and you are waiting to do the same, you insert yourself to become the service worker's focus. Believe me, they want you to intervene almost every time. You also, do not have to be blatantly rude to do so. In the south, we call these a polite nudge of dismissal. You accomplish such, by smiling and greeting the service worker with, 'Good Morning/Afternoon' the proceed to step forward to begin your transaction. Be prepared, sometimes this ploy works, but at other times The Gabber will turn on you. Again, politeness is a good way to diffuse the situation with this personality.

    While they want to be the center of attention, they do not want to be seen as a problem in most cases. You can stop their tirade if they turn on you by saying something along the lines of, 'I do apologize, but I have a pressing matter I need to attend to when I leave here.' It is not the best of excuses, but it does have a tendency to ring true with them, as they feel most things they do have significant importance. Whether that is true or not, fate can decide.

An alternative to the polite nudge is the outright confrontation. Calling them out amongst lines of other people or shoppers has a rather bracing effect. Also, it should be noted, this particular method will get you a scathing dressing down, but in some cases where you've had a bad day and need to release some steam, it is welcome. True, it will end in a verbal sparring match of veritable influence to the people around you, but can serve as a reminder that the world does not revolve singularly around The Gabber in question.

In the final scenario, The Gabber is a fellow employee. These situations are a bit more touchy, because you will not only be diffusing this particular individual, but the person they were actively speaking of. This is not an exaggeration. Sadly, when you work with someone with the Gabber mentality, they will actively run their mouth about the people on staff. Whether it is true or not, makes no difference. They will cause discord and upheaval, much like one would see a Gabber do at a family reunion like mentioned earlier.

These situations will be harder to handle. When emotions run high, especially on the clock, people get irritable. This in turn bleeds over to the other people around them. If you do not shut this down early in the shift, the people you are working with will become more and more irate. This will result in poor performance, a slew of mistakes, and in some cases – bad service for your customers.

Your best bet, and truly your only hope, is to get the situation shut down before it starts. One way is to keep your Gabber personality in a solo position where they have very little interaction with other employees or customers. While this may sound cruel, or like you're setting them apart, it is not. In truth, you're giving them less distractions to get their job done and done well – while also making sure the rest of the staff is not pulled in to some cyclone of drama.

However, this tactic is not always effective and the gossip train will begin. If that happens, reminding everyone that you have work to do can stamp out any repeating of these conversations. Other effective ways, are to pull the Gabber aside and remind them that work is not the place to discuss other issues, especially not those of others on staff. However, that may not work either, so one may have to resort to having The Gabber sent home from their shift with a verbal reprimand and then addressing the problem with the rest of the staff to stop the same event from happening again.

Be aware. This will not do you any favors among the staff, or even with the Gabber in question. To some, it may seem a bit harsh. Others may applaud it, but be fully aware that taking this route will do you no favors because it will signify that you are set apart from the rest of the employees.

If you are one of the employees and you encounter a Gabber doing these things – you can stop it by letting management know. Any manager worth their salt will address the situation and have it nipped in the bud quickly. Just be very aware of the choices you make in handling these situations, because each have their own downfall.

# CHAPTER 10
# HATORADE

Sadly, something that has to be addressed when you speak about customer service in general is hate.

No, not the generalized meaning of the word, but a soul-crushing, unrelenting wave of darker emotion that pours out of people whether they mean to express it or not. In recent decades we have seen this emotion manifest in some horrible ways: road rage, school shootings, riots, fires, murders, hate crimes, etc. This list goes on and on.

One thing no one talks about, is how much of it people see in the customer service industry. There is no shortage of stories and scenarios that people give time and again that underline the bad behavior of people in public situations where their hatred bleeds through.

It is bad enough that the need to write this chapter to clear up misconceptions is undeniable. Sadly, we have become a society that finds fault in everything. Politically correctness has become it's own monster and overtaken everything around us because the smallest action, look, or word seems to set people off.

It can be agreed that there were some things in the world that needed to change.

However, this time we have gone too far. Hatred now runs deep and lines have been drawn that make it hard for anyone to function in society without feeling the pressure of others judging their every move and word. A simple mispronunciation, or misused word, can now incite a slew of vitriol in this modern age with camera phones and social media platforms.

For people working in Customer Service it is ten times worse. While it cannot be said the different stores and restaurants that these scenarios have come out of, you can be sure that they come from places like you visit every single day. Rest assured these come from retail stores, drug stores, restaurants, food trucks, and a slew of other places which offer services to the general public. The sad part is, along with these services, the populace is given a new target to mete out their frustrations and hatred on. The workers.

While it would be nice to tell people that this does not happen, it would be a lie. Especially since the pandemic, the general attitude among the public has gotten far more aggressive and loud. People are angrier, afraid of change and what it all means. In turn, they take this out on those who are the easiest to target.

Sadly, the people they target are in a situation that leaves them unable to defend themselves or talk back. Yes, their are subtle ways to try and shore up their defense, but company policies leave them unable to really do anything. Society has gotten to a ludicrous point where the motto 'the customer is always right' is a blanket statement allowing people to mistreat and abuse customer service workers across the board. It has become the equivalent of what people believe to be a get out of jail free card, when in truth it has started a trend so disgusting that many businesses are turning to new policies throw that statement out the window.

Allowing people to use this loophole for years to abuse workers has caused a shortage in people willing to work in service positions across the board. That particular phrase becoming a blanket statement to allow people in society to take out old habits and prejudices on the people trying to help them has only served to foster more hatred, in the workers themselves. Witnessing anyone going from a hopeful, willing student with goals on what they would accomplish with the pay from a new job – to a despondent and almost violent personality that hates their workplace and interacting with people as whole is crippling. Knowing you can also do very little to change it is disheartening.

This growing trend has caused a plethora of changes to the industry in recent years. A system of change that has society complaining about them and demanding better customer service from the companies.

Yet, how are these employers supposed to give the people what they ask for? Between the low rate of the wages, the treatment these workers get from the employer and customers alike, we are seeing a changing dynamic in the infrastructure of these businesses.

More so, the lack of people willing to enter the service industry. Today, we have access to the internet and daily we see small videos or stories on social media of people attacking customer service workers in different ways. Some of these attacks are founded on long held prejudices or hatreds that simmer beneath the surface. Others are born of sheer frustration and angst over things not being exactly the way they should be. And yet more, are propagated by nothing more than fear of change or the unknown.

No matter the reason, when these attacks happen, there is a picture of hatred and rage that is projected to not only the person who is attacked, but the world. These attacks foster and grow a sentiment that others will fall in line with. Humans, on the whole, need interaction and the validation of others like them. So, when such an event occurs, there is a divide that becomes apparent as people take sides, either with the employee being attacked, or the person who attacked them justifying it. This breeds a new frustration and a new hate, that begins the cycle a new.

This cycle fosters keeping people thinking in the same way their grandfather's did. They foster an ongoing prejudice that would have died out before, but now flares back to life as people argue that the situation is the cause of ethnicity, religion, race, belief. Whatever it takes to justify the action or reaction.

And we allow it.

Yet, in schools, we tell our children that they matter. That no one has the right to degrade or demean them, making them feel less than. However, as an example, we turn around and do exactly those things to individuals that are just trying to earn an honest wage.

As if it is not bad enough to witness these happenings in social media – one must consider the workers who are out there every day. These individuals live and breathe these experiences first hand every hour they are on the clock. Yet, we laugh at these videos and shake our heads as if they are truly some form of entertainment.

There is no excuse for a person to be subjected to the things we ask customer service workers to put up with. No one would ask their child to take a job where random people would walk up to them and call them stupid or idiotic. Nor would we condone them being placed before a crowd and made a mockery of for their appearance or the task they are doing. Yet, we continue to do so to the other people working in these businesses.

People that have consulted or shared their stories for this book, have witnessed first hand the insults that society had bestowed upon these workers. There is no shortage of monikers, names, or quips that have been thrown in these workers faces and shouted at the top of their lungs. There are pages upon pages on Facebook dedicated to embarrassing or shaming these workers to the rest of the world. It is sickening.

Truly, a little kindness would go a long way. On both sides. Make no mistake, despite a history in customer service for the last five years, there is a healthy amount of disrespect among the workers for customers too. None of this is right. None of this is what we should be holding to as a society.

Frustration is understandable, no matter what side of the line you are on. However, it is when that frustration becomes something volatile and insulting that it becomes a problem. Allowing anger to settle within you and spark a rage centered around any former prejudice or preconceived notion is only setting us up for failure for the whole of society. Hell, maybe even humanity.

If ever you find yourself in a situation that is escalating, try and remove yourself immediately. As a customer service worker, call over a manager and let them handle the situation as best they are able. Try not to take the words they yell at you to heart. Be kind, remember everyone is under a different type of stress, and it comes out in weird and sometimes unsettling ways.

For customers, please be aware that the person trying to help you is under pressure as well. They want to be accurate at their job and sometimes that job is dependent upon such accuracy. There is also no guarantee that these workers will be able to help you in exactly the way you want. That is not their fault, and please understand that they will do all they can to help you with what information they do have.

Remember, whichever side of this you stand on, kindness will go a long way. Everyone needs to let go of their preconceived notions and be more understanding of others. Until we do that, there will be no lacking in the amount of hateful encounters. When we make the choice to be better, to do better and be more accepting of things, everything will improve for the better. In both these workplaces and for the customers shopping in them.

## CHAPTER 11
## IMPOSSIBLE ASKS

What is an Impossible Ask?

Let me tell you, it is one of the most unpleasant things to ever deal with. If it could be said that things like this only happen on the level of a company office to an outer branch with the lowest employee, this would not even be mention-able.

However, a book on customer service, means that this particular subject is actually kind of a big deal. In this particular field of work it is improbable that you will not encounter at least one situation that is not able to be handled perfectly – if it can be handled at all. While it would be lovely to say you could and would handle every situation, scenario, or question brought to you in this field, the sad truth is you will not be able to handle each and every one. No matter what people tell you, or the training you receive, there will inevitably come a day where you cannot handle a situation because someone asks you to do the impossible.

Surprisingly, these requests will not come from where you would think. Only about ten percent of your impossible asks will be from your customer base. All of the rest will come from either your staff, or your employer themselves. The worst part about this, especially if you enter customer service management at any point – is the knowledge that it is their own math that is wrong because what they are asking for is not practical to the normal work environment.

As mentioned in previous chapters, every company in customer service – whether retail or food – is only worried about the bottom line. For them, that is maximizing profit. In a society where the inflation is causing a constant uptick in the cost of items, production, and shipping the only way to mitigate these rising costs is in two categories for employers at the store level. That is inventory and labor. Sadly, those who work in corporate offices, crunch numbers and come up with plans to help maximize profit, that are not always feasible or in some cases, are detrimental to the actual customer service part of things. These are where many of your impossible asks come from.

These tasks are born of the ideas of office jockeys who have zero clue how things function at the store level. Since personal experience has been in the food service industry with a couple of pizza chains, they will be the examples I use in this chapter. Do not misunderstand, there will be examples of customers making impossible asks too. It is imperative for the public to understand why certain decisions are being made in these stores that are changing how they operate and impact their experiences.

The problem with an impossible ask, is that no matter what steps you take to meet the parameters set before you, it will be unobtainable. In the late 80's and early 90's we saw one such example among Pizza Franchises with the 'delivery in 30 minutes or less.' This movement sparked a huge dip in profit for many companies, because there are too many factors to try and control. Mind you, this was before the time of cell phone apps, and online ordering. This was when you had to call in your order and place it with the store.

    Now, thinking outside of the normal customer perspective, lets shift your focus. Imagine you are standing at the counter, the phone rings and you answer it. There is a customer and they want to order five pizzas with a couple of sodas. No big deal. You put their order in and hang up the phone. But then it rings a second time. This time, it's a customer who wants one pizza and three orders of wings. Again, should be simple enough. You put the order in and tell them it will be ready in twenty minutes for pick up. None of this seems too difficult. After all, there should be someone else over on the make line to make the food, and then you can catch the oven because the phone is quiet. Seems simple enough.

    Which is the catch. Most business models for these companies do not consider the fact you need people to perform carry out and perform excellent customer service. The reality of this scenario in current time, is that on top of those two orders you took by phone, there are four more orders that came in over the internet. In the best of scenarios, the internet is on a fifteen minute delay to update. So while you move to help make the six orders now on the screen, other people looking on the internet to order, aren't aware that you have a back up on orders. The apps and websites will still tell your customers there is only a fifteen minute wait for carry out or a thirty minute wait for delivery, so six more orders appear.

Now, you only have yourself and one other person in store. The two of you, are supposed to make all the food on the screen, and catch the oven. Let's be generous and give you a delivery driver that can catch the oven for you. So, two making food, one person catching food and cutting it on the cut table to get the order's organized and routed where they need to be. Now, the front door to the store opens, the bell rings, you greet the person walking into the store while you are making a pizza to get in the oven. The orders on the screen are piling up, and you are getting two new orders for every one you clear.

Now, you have a person in the lobby. Your driver is scrambling to catch the pizzas and put them together in orders. The other person making food with you is busily attacking the next item that needs to be made. The door opens again, another customer enters, then the bell for the pick up window goes off.

At this point, even with three people, there aren't enough hands for the work that has to be done. The phone starts to ring again, and there is no one else to answer the phone. The customers in the lobby get restless and are tired of waiting. The second phone starts to ring. As horrifying as this sounds, it is all true. This scenario happens nearly everyday in restaurants across the country. It happens in grocery stores and retail stores as well. While I cannot pinpoint the problems in retail stores for you because I'm sure things have changed in the last decade, it is safe to say they are facing business models much like the ones we see in food service.

  While it varies across franchises and types of restaurants, most food service jobs are run from corporate offices. The sad part of this is these people have no idea of the intricacies of running a restaurant smoothly. What it takes, or how things quickly snowball to a point that service suffers. This is where impossible asks begin.

  The first part of the impossible ask comes from the folly of these people in the offices setting the rules and limits for the stores below them. This first ask, is to have the store managers cut labor and reduce the people on their payroll with higher salaries. They eliminate overtime for everyone and then expect these general manager to find people willing to work harder for less money – all while keeping the customers satisfied and business flowing smoothly.

While the only business model that I can reference for you deals with pizza service and delivery, many food service companies are in the same boat. The business model chosen for most pizza companies focuses on maximizing profits by paying the least amount they can in staffing and labor costs. Considering the rising costs of products to make their food, the only way to cut corners in these areas is through labor. So, when you have an employee who is a manager, but they make four to five dollars over minimum wage the people in the cushy corner office tell you to start filling those hours with delivery drivers, or new hires in order to cut the labor cost in half. More so, they budget out your schedule, assigning you a certain amount of hours to schedule your employees with. Sadly, this schedule is grossly ineffective.

The biggest folly in these schedules falls on their refusal to count orders customers make for Carry Out or Pick Up, effective. While yes, there can be plenty of blame laid on the fact they expect many of these franchises to hire employees at 7.25 an hour and expect them to run every single facet of the store including food preparation is also a bit mistake. However, in teh overall consensus, the numbers they crunch are only focused on the labor needed to handle delivery.

Most businesses using this model, run into common problems. Like, pushing to make orders for the public and while they are trying to do so, being unable to answer phones or go to the counter to help customers coming to pick up their orders. This is a common complaint spread across restaurants and franchises across the country. Now, you will understand why. When they take into account the sales a business does, they do not count the carry out aspect side of the business. They look at the sales generated in delivery and use that to plan their schedule.

    The issue with this restriction, is that it limits the ability of a business to actually provide great customer service. What you get instead, is a bunch of workers pressed into trying to fulfill orders, with not enough hands, and unable to break away from those orders to handle counters and the like. This results in customers complaining about the service they receive, such as not being greeted, having to wait to receive their order, or the ever popular being rushed and the employee was curt and short with them. It's a domino effect and one that never plays over well.

    The scheduling these businesses allow, have a multitude of driver hours available, but stipulate the there can only be 2 or 3 insiders for maybe two hours to cover two thousand in sales. The problem with this is, people order what they want. They like variety. So catering to that takes some work. Most nights, those two people allowed to be there to cook or make food, one of them is the on duty manager, having to multitask. So it again, leaves no one to greet and handle customers coming to pick up their food or order.

The reason this is an impossible ask, is because all of these stores, the general manager and the assistant managing staff they have, are asked to perform monumental tasks to their own detriment. These people are expected to do the jobs of two or three others while maintaining a bright, shiny attitude for the customers and keeping service running smoothly. Keep in mind, they must also route deliveries, handle employee concerns, balance inventory, keep money secure, lock the store down, and a slew of other responsibilities that come with the position on a good day. Now, they are being asked to short staff themselves, and send people home, to take on the task of making all the food the store is producing for both carry out and delivery.

What makes this an impossible ask, is that no one person, no matter how much training or skill they have, is capable of juggling so many hats without something falling through. While it is horrible to say, the choice that they are forced to make, is the discomfort of the few in support of the many. Since many of these businesses teach you that pleasing a customer that is remote and does not see you, is harder than pleasing the ones directly before you, the choice is not really yours on what and how you handle these situations. It is far better to make a push to please ten customers that you don't see by finishing all of the orders on screen before you approach the customers waiting at the counter, then to move away from making food and delay the orders of several customers at once. This situation is and remains a no-win scenario. Therefore, it is impossible to accomplish.

  Another example of an impossible ask when dealing with corporate offices versus local stores is the ratio of pay to the work being done. It can be argued that American Capitalism is a major part of what gave birth to the idea of the American Dream. Sadly, that also meant that society changed the rules in regard to how such a thing was accomplished, and in essence, began to phase out the lifestyle of anyone considered blue collar or less than that. Poverty is now being redefined daily, and people who twenty years ago were considered working class, are now considered less than poor. The ability to make the almighty dollar mean more, has made the system itself more corrupt. No longer can you work just one job to make ends meet, but instead push for a high paying corporate job, or work several blue collar jobs crammed into a simple week long schedule. This particular truth can be seen in this part of Impossible Asks.

  The average minimum wage required for cost of living is considered to be seven dollars and twenty-five cents. In more than half the states in America, this is the minimum wage they set as the standard. However, this is not a feasible or reasonable wage to live off of. The problem is, while this is the minimum, those in positions higher then that, are being paid to scale with them, but all of these roles, from the minimum wage hourly employee, to the top of their particular store, suffer more burdens than ever before.

No, I am not trying to tour that corporate America is evil, but there is a serious hole in the structure of our financial society. That hole can be blatantly seen in the customer service industry as a whole. The issue that most face is that they only see the people who work in the corporate offices of said companies, and the pay they get for brainstorming about what or how to effect change in the stores below them that actually offer the services. More than that, these lower echelons, the stores that are actually part of the daily life of the public are where they cut costs and do the most damage. To explain this, let's begin at the top of the local store, shall we?

While it varies for retail service, in food service, a local store begins with the GM or General Manager. These individuals oversee the whole staff of the store. While many believe they are paid per hour, the truth is in ninety percent of these stores, GM's are the one and only salaried employee at the local level. Most of these contracts state, that the GM works fifty hours a week for a set amount of pay. That pay varies from place to place, but in most cases, the average when broken down works out to be about fourteen to fifteen dollars an hour. These managers are also offered the incentive perk of getting a bonus if the store runs in profit per period or whatever scale the company uses to get through the year. These bonuses can be by period, month, quarter, or annually dependent on the terms of the company in question. While this may sound somewhat lucrative, there is of course the hidden expectations and agendas.

So, what exactly is the rub so to speak?

General Managers are contracted to work fifty hours a week. Yet, when they are asked to cut labor or save money by their superiors, or in some cases, flat out ordered to do so, who makes up the loss in productivity? When you cut two to three people from a shift, but have to continue keeping service up and running, that responsibility fall on the GM. So, they end up staying, working sixty to seventy hours a week in order to cover pitfalls. The problem with this? It's free labor.

If anyone were to ask an hourly employee to work over forty hours a week and not get paid extra or just generally paid for their time, it would be an uproar. The better business bureau and labor bureau would be called stating that a company is in violation of decent, civil rights afforded to employees. Yet, when someone who will only get paid for fifty hours, works more than that, they see no benefit, no pay, no reward to reap. They can only hope, what they are doing is enough to keep their store in enough profit that they will get a percentage of it at the end of the billing cycle or period. More than that, these GM's now have to balance a list of tasks that come with running a store up to a corporate standard (no matter how unreasonable it is) with doing the jobs of one to two other hourly employees. Basically, they are doing three to four different jobs on top of their own in order to obey the dictates sent down from someone sitting in an office who has no idea or clue how their store or shop actually operates.

      Under the GM, you have Assistant Managers. These employees are commonly dismissed by most. Both their corporate higher ups and the public have a tendency to snark and overlook these employees as middle men with no idea how to run or operate the store. It does not matter if they have more training then an hourly employee. All others see is someone who is not at the top of the food chain, trying to mitigate and handle the problems of the store. Doing so when they are also asked to run with one or two less people then they should have due to trying to trim the budget with labor. These assistants must now learn to take on multiple roles much like a GM does. They are paid for their time, but because of the strictures placed by their corporate office, cannot get overtime. They are also required to run their shift, despite hang ups and a lack of personnel without a flaw. This is something that is utterly improbable to accomplish. Being short on staff, means there are holes in the process of making and serving food to the customers. More than that, these assistant managers have to be ready to step in and assume multiple roles for themselves, despite being told they would have support. Their own GM unable to offer them help because they cannot allow others to have overtime or a lack of hours available in the schedule since the company does not allow you to have labor coverage for carry out.

These strictures also mean that any manager, be they assistant or GM, who is trying to run a shift and has an employee call out for whatever reason, cannot replace them. You have to forge ahead and operate with what you have. More often then not, in these scenarios, you will see the Manager on Duty, running from one task, to another. They will greet you, take your order, answer the phone, take that order, wash their hands, try to start making food, get orders in the oven, take another order, run to the drive thru to pass an order to a customer, then move about in a wild circle trying to do fifty things right in front of you.

The worst part is, they can't just stop. Say no. Refuse to do any of those things, and why? Because they are there to serve the customers, even if they seem to keep making the customers angry. And all this... is just to the lower management level. Now, we move on to the final tier...

Hourly Employees.

To be general and hurry this chapter along, we will not give these employees specific titles. Instead, let's just be clear that it includes everyone from delivery drivers to cooks and wait staff. That way we can cover the whole of the group. Now, for seven twenty0five an hour, we now expect these employee to shoulder the weight of their own job, plus those of others. It is not uncommon to see cooks acting as wait staff, or even delivery drivers because of stores forced to cut staff. Most people, are trying to be sure they get close to forty hours a week, even if this is a side job to help pay bills. Now, they are expected to not only do the job they were hired to do, but more on top of it. These hourly employees will do jobs that a majority of the populace will curl their nose and sneer at, saying that no job could pay them enough to clean up a bathroom after other people. Yet, these hourly employees that they sneer and jeer at, are expected to do so. They are also tasked with cleaning the floors, walls, and storage facilities within the restaurant. Handling customers, their orders, and their money in order to keep the flow of traffic moving through the store. Take out garbage, wash dishes, sweep and mop floors, sanitize surfaces and restock for the opening crew or closing crew dependent on what shift they work.

Yet, as a society we tout that we should pay people for the jobs they do, then decry paying food service workers more because 'they don't do anything.' Then when a business is unable to hire employees because they are told what will be expected of them for such a paltry sum, complain to their corporate headquarters and get the whole of the store in hot water because we expect more for less money. It's ridiculous.

One would not ask a computer programmer to work his job and that of the marketing group without some incentive of pay. Yet, the expectation of both society and corporate offices, expects exactly that of the employees that can be found at the store level. From the GM on down. So again, an Impossible Ask, since no person will tolerate doing so much work for so little pay for an extended amount of time. They may take the job to tide them over, but the minute something else becomes available, even if it is only for a dollar more, they will leave. It is to be expected and is something that will not change until the wages do.

While the impossible asks above are more an outline of why what the companies ask of their employees is impossible. There are some demands that are impossible which come from customers. Sometimes these are simple enough to explain and handle. Other times, not so much.

Impossible asks on the customer service side of things fall into two categories. Those that are completely impossible to perform, and those that cannot be met right now due to a lack of product or availability. While many people believe that nothing is impossible, there are certain matters in which this is entirely true.

Take being in a pizza restaurant for instance. Despite what people may want to believe, it is impossible to make a pizza that has half one sauce, and half another. When the sauce is heated in the oven, whether it is tomato or cheese based, begins to melt and spread. In the center they will overlap one another and cause some rather nasty combinations to occur. So you cannot accurately make that pizza for anyone. The same goes for a pizza that has cheese on one half and not the other. This request will be impossible always. No matter the store or franchise, the cheese that is used to make these products is shredded. Even if you focus on only putting that cheese on half of the pizza, when it melts, it spreads to the side that is supposed to be without. While you would think that such a thing is not a big deal, if you have one customer that is lactose intolerant and just a small bit of that cheese makes it to the other side of the pizza, you will regret the outcome.

  To be completely honest, trying to tell any customer that what they are asking for is not possible is a monumental task. Especially to do so and still try to find a way to make them happy. It is a delicate balance, but most times it is possible. When it is not, you will have to resign yourself o being cursed and yelled at, through no fault of your own.

  The other kind of impossible ask, dealing with a lack of product or items. Sometimes when you encounter an impossible ask, it is due to someone asking for something that you cannot get a hold of or is not available. While these are typically resolved quickly enough, they can be difficult to handle when in full swing. Customers do not always understand that we cannot control the amount of items that are available or shipped to the store. Especially since COVID with losses in production and lack of food products due to losses in the farming and processing communities.

These situations can be resolved over time. Sometimes, there will be difficulties in handling them, but they will pass. Just be aware, that sometimes, you cannot always accomplish what people ask you for. It's okay to say that these tasks are impossible, or unable to be completed. Just be aware, these can happen and are very real.

# CHAPTER 12
# JUSTIFICATION JAN

As you have noticed we are running through this manual alphabetically, and before we get to the subject that reigns over social media nowadays, we have one more stop.

Justification Jan.

This is the hardest type of personality not to loose your cool with. They exist in every aspect of the customer service realm. You will encounter them as customers, as employees, and even as an employer. There is no place you can look where you will not find a Justification Jan present and waiting.

While yes, sometimes a person will feel the need to justify their choice or actions. A Justification Jan has this trait to the extreme. The smallest action they make, require a long drawn out explanation as to why or how it was done. This can be tedious as well as time consuming for anyone dealing with it. Sadly, when you encounter such a personality, it has a tendency to put an already on edge person over the line. This personality is also the cause of many miscommunications between people that are moving in the world of customer service on a daily basis.

As a customer, you will encounter a Justification Jan in any situation where you have a complaint. While yes, sometimes you want an explanation for why or how something you bought or acquired was messed up, there will be one person in the line of people you will talk to that will be a Justification Jan. Sometimes, it will be the manager handling your complaint. In other instances it will be the employee you first came in contact with. Whichever one you encounter, the general conversation will remain the same.

A Justification Jan will find any minute excuse to explain away what happened and say that it was to be expected. It will not matter if you have ordered or acquired the same item before without a hitch, these particular people will explain it in a way that says you would have had the problem often for whatever reason they focus in on. While a manager is required to try and straighten out an issue and make it right, most times, they will tell you that the occurrence is a one time thing or something uncommon. Unless they are a Justification Jan.

With a Justification Jan, the situation becomes a blame on banality and the mundane. Whatever your issue was, they make it a federal case and proceed to pinpoint a singular happenstance that will ALWAYS cause the item in question to be wrong. There will be a lack of 'I'm Sorry' and a whole lot of, 'the reason this happens.' As if your complaint is something that is inevitable, even if that is not completely and totally accurate.

The problem with a Justification Jan is that they will always believe that the choices they made or the actions they enacted were the ONLY recourse in the situation. Despite the fact that in most situations there will be any of ten million other ways to accomplish what they or the customer want, you will not be able to convince them of that.

When you are a customer dealing with a manager like this, the best thing you can do, is just ask for a simplistic remake or replacement. If they are even more adamant, you can ask for a different manager, or the store manager. The truth is, while yes most places that deal with customer service are limiting the options for fixing or replacing items, they still want to be sure you are satisfied as long as the cost of the fix is within reason. This is where the Justification Jan is a problem. Something will be impossible to do accurately, such as the two different sauces or no cheese on one side examples above, but not everything that you ask for will be. The Justification Jan will argue their point to try and force you into something they consider simpler, and in that moment, going higher up the chain will be warranted.

Now, when dealing with a Justification Jan as a customer, there will be moments you want to scream. This is not a maybe scenario, but a definitive absolute. When dealing with the Justification Jan as a customer, they will argue incessantly that whatever the problem you are trying to fix, they are not at fault. A perfect example exists in food service, period. The problem with one of these personalities as a customer comes when they do not understand why it is you are not responsible for their experience. Sadly, most times you will have to fix it, costing your store and company money when it is the customer themselves who are at fault.

For instance, let us set the scene. You work in food service and an order comes in online. As is expected, you make the food, box it for presentation, double check that you have everything put together and place it in the warmer to wait for the customer to pick it up.

An hour passes by, the food remains in the warmer, but you have noticed several other orders come and go. You try to call the customer, thinking perhaps they have forgotten their order or went to the wrong location. You get no answer. So now, you wait.

And wait.

And wait some more.

At the hour and a half mark, you remove the food from the warmer and dispose of it per protocol. Old food is not acceptable, and anything after forty-five minutes is considered sub-par in quality and food safety. So, you dispose of it and go about your business.

Finally, three hours after the order was made, a person walks into your store. And the conversation goes a little something like this:

**You:** Welcome to Food Palace! Are you here to pick up or place an order today?

**Jan:** I'm here to Pick Up an order. The name is J.J.

**You:** I see, well I do apologize but we do not have your food ready. We can have it done in about fifteen minutes.

**Jan:** I already ordered, how do you not have my food?

**You:** Your order was placed at eleven-thirty. It is now two-thirty. We had to throw the food out when it had been held in the window for too long.

**Jan:** I better receive a discount since I have to wait.

**You:** Ma'am. I do apologize but there will be no discount today, we will gladly remake your food fresh, but we have to follow proto-

**Jan:** You will give me a discount. You don't have my food ready after I already ordered. I shouldn't have to pay because you can't do your job.

**You:** Ma'am, again, I apologize your food is not ready, but we are not supposed to keep food longer than an hour.

**Jan:** I had things to do. It is your job to have my food ready when I show up.

**You:** I understand that, ma'am. However, I have to follow the rules to be sure your food is not a danger to you or others. Again, I apologize for the inconvenience but it won't take us long to remake your order.

*Jan:* So what you're telling me is I paid money to get nothing and you won't even discount my food because you messed up? I want to speak to the manager.

*You:* I am the manager on duty at the moment, ma'am. And you will get the food you paid for, hot and fresh out of the oven. Again, I apologize for the inconvenience, but we don't want to give our customers food that could put them at risk.

*Jan:* Is there a manager here above you? Can I speak to them? Your customer service is bad and you should give me something for the fact you threw away my food.

*You:* There is a manager above me, but they are not here at the moment. You are more than welcome to call my manager Healani when she is here tomorrow.

*Jan:* This is unacceptable. I had errands I needed to run and you just threw my food away and won't even give me a discount for the inconvenience.

*You:* I understand that, ma'am. I am more than happy to remake the fresh food and while I apologize for the inconvenience of having to wait, I am more than happy to throw in a two liter drink or some cinnabread for the trouble.

*Jan:* No, I want my food and a discount now. You had no right to throw away my food that I had already paid for. You should have kept it here waiting for me.

*You:* Again, I apologize. We did try to call to see when you would arrive to make sure your food would be ready but we could not reach you on the phone.

***Jan:*** I was out running errands. How are you going to call me when I'm not home? You're saying it's my fault you don't have my food.

***You:*** No, ma'am. Just that we want you to have the best experience possible instead of old food that has been left sitting on the rack for -

***Jan:*** You just get me my food. I have never felt so disrespected. You will be sure I'll be calling your boss in the morning and making sure they know about your service. Throwing out a paying customers food, you should be ashamed of yourself. We work hard for the money we pay you, the least you could do is have our food ready.

It is to be noted, that this argument will continue if you let it. The best thing to be done, is to give them their order, plus something extra to try and smooth it over. Be aware, that likely won't work either and they will call back the next day to complain. As long as you stick to the company standards, there will be no fault found in how you handle the situation. As you can see, no matter where the conversation turned, Jan made it seem like the fault lay on the worker, and not on the decisions she herself made. In a situation like that, you have to resign yourself to being their bad guy and be as polite as possible while you enforce the guidelines given by your employer.

All in all, these personalities are difficult to manager no matter the situation you find yourself in. Your best bet, is to remain cool, calm, and collected through the encounter in order to negate any possible backlash from the interaction. Yes, a Justification Jan will work your nerves even under the best of circumstances. Still, they can only get as far as you will let them. By no means should you bow out, and give them exactly what they are asking for every single time, but a little bit of patience can go a long way to making sure you diffuse the time bomb of their personality before it becomes an even larger issue, no matter where you stand in the situation with them. Boss, Friend, Employee, Customer, or Bystander you can control the situation a lot more easily by letting them speak and being as level-headed as you can manage.

## CHAPTER 13
## KARENS – THE NIGHTMARE

Our next subject is one I believe everyone should have expected.

With the rise of social media in our society, we have also seen the emergence of an entirely new breed of customer or personality. One that is so disruptive and quite frankly disgusting, there is no way to dismiss them or pretend they do not exist or make an impact on the world of customer service. Sadly, their influence is not limited to these areas. In recent months and years, it has expanded past the customer service industry where they were most prevalent to encompassing the wide spectrum of interaction of general public gatherings or movement.

That personality is – the Karen.

Karen's, while they may seem to be a relatively new phenomenon, have actually been around for years. Sadly, in that time, society was polite enough and had a better understanding of general decency that actually experiencing a Karen was something few and far between. In today's society, finding a new video that has some kind of situation with a person facing off versus a Karen is a daily occurrence. What had once been a fleeting encounter every blue moon, has become a commonplace staple taking place in everyone's day to day lives.

Much as it would be nice to state that these encounters are something to be looked over, that is not the case. This sense of complete entitlement and judgment that Karen's spew over the masses is disgusting. While it would be wonderful to have skipped them as a topic, because of the outrageous behavior of some of these people, it warranted a mention.

Why, you may ask?

Despite the fact it is galling to acknowledge, everyone encounters a Karen at some point. The appearance of the Karen has surpassed that of a being one just encountered while in the service industry but instead becoming a disruptive and damaging presence that is encountered in everyday life. It is this simple fact that makes it necessary to mention the Karen personality here. Not just as a guideline for dealing with such a being in the service industry, but in how anyone should interact with said Karen when they are confronted with one.

As most will be aware, the Karen is almost always a creature that is filled with a sense of entitlement. The people with these types of personalities think everything that they do or say is part of some righteous cause. Further, they believe that all other people should curtail to their every whim or demand. The Karen is known to be rude, aggressive, bossy, argumentative, narrow-minded, and dramatic – just to name a few of the traits that one commonly witness when in contact with one of these people. More often than not, those who share this personality lash out over insignificant details and will often be seen as the aggressors in any situation where they confront others.

People with this personality are often small-minded and completely unable to listen to the opinions or beliefs of other individuals. They believe whole-heartedly that they are correct in everything they do and say – and therefore have the right to pressure and bully others. More often then not, these persons will lash out irrationally and become a nuisance of detrimental proportions to those around them. While some would argue that this is an exaggeration, recent months have shown with a rapidly growing number of viral videos and clips – that this type of behavior has become a daily thing in our world.

There is no longer a single day that passes without a Karen of some sort getting their five minutes of fame because of these actions. These individuals, with their sense of entitlement and righteous fury are shown harassing others on a daily basis. They cause scenes that are completely uncalled for and can be seen as fully offensive to anyone with a half-decent moral code. Time and again, we are subjected to their narrow-minded views and demands. Forced to witness their ire as they are delivered en masse as screaming rants unleashed on unsuspecting people that these Karen's see as a threat.

Ten years ago, it was bad enough when all these personalities had to unleash their vitriol upon were service workers. Now, however, they have expanded, folding in their rather questionable objectives and beliefs to their entitlement which has garnered an absolute for them that the world at large should bow to their wants, needs, and whims when they deliver one of their patent rants. Since the innovation of technology and phone apps, we have seen Karen's start to confront random strangers over the most superfluous things. Some going so far as to use their position in society or their general position whatsoever to racially profile anyone that does not share the same skin tone as them.

Where before these individuals would attack, scream, and insult the people of the customer and food service industry, they now accost perfect strangers on the street. They pop up at the weekly soccer game and scream bloody murder because a child's parents are not of the same race and should not be allowed to attend the game. Or on the street, harassing people walking their dogs in public parks before then threatening them with police action if they do not choose to leave said park just because the Karen demands it.

Still, you have others who have gone so far as to camp outside of the homes of other citizens, demanding they leave the place of residence because it is believed that they do not belong as part of that neighborhoods demographic. Other videos surface, with some woman screaming at a man that he should hand over his son's phone because he stole it from someone else, with no proof of that act on record. A phone which, is proven later to belong to said child even after the person in question has pushed and screamed and threatened that child while trying to snatch said phone repeatedly.

Yes, Karen's have become a literal disease that plague society daily. Whether it is acknowledged or not, people that have this personality are extremely difficult to handle. In all honesty, they are explosive and have a tendency to bring out the worst in anyone forced to be in their presence.

Sadly, this particular personality is also the most difficult one to handle without getting oneself in trouble. In truth, there are very few people able to handle such a person because their attacks are viciously slighted to demean and degrade anyone. More than that, the sense of superiority these Karen's feel, makes them believe they are untouchable. As such, they act without thinking there will be any consequences on their part, making them a danger to any and everyone around them.

Dealing with Karen's is old hat to anyone who works in the service industry, but by no means is it easy. More than one worker has lost their job in the face of such a confrontation, and sadly they will not be the last. Karen's have become the mythical creature of the deep, given life with the specific purpose of challenging the world with their presence. In most instances, encounters with them are a validation of the age old adage, 'what doesn't kill you makes you stronger.' Just in watching the videos that you encounter online, it becomes clear that Karen's are vicious, vindictive, and completely focused on destroying anyone and anything in their path. Surviving an encounter with a Karen without catching a charge, or losing your job is the only win there is in the scenario.

Before we get down to the examples, it should be noted that these encounters take their toll on you. No matter your position in these scenarios, the emotional and mental exasperation that comes with these encounters can and will be detrimental. There will always be lasting effects and in most cases a kind of incredulity at the sheer audacity of the person you dealt with. Their barbed insults and sly comments will be difficult to withstand, especially when they become personal. Make no mistake, standing your ground in any way versus a Karen will bring out her monstrous side. Every single flaw or judgment that they can make will become ammo and be spoken into existence.

Part of the reason it galls me as a writer to mention the Karen is because of this trait in particular. As a person, I cannot stand others that are cruel just for the sake of being cruel. Especially when they do so over something as asinine as not enough salt on their food or something similar. The existence of this type of personality underlines the complete and abject lack of common human decency in today's society. The people that have this personality are the worst type of people by definition. The reason I say this, is because they use their own personal hatreds, biases, or moral definitions to try and justify their treatment of others. We have long passed a time where we stood in beliefs that someone's worth was measured by the color of their skin, or their choice of religion. Yet, these Karen personalities, use those very concepts to single out and attack others over small inconsistencies or dislikes they encounter in everyday life. It is a despicable practice and one that keeps hatred alive in our social environment. Such things should not be tolerated even for amusement.

  Secondly, people who make assumptions about others are a huge part of what is wrong with our world today. Karen personalities live and thrive on making assumptions about everyone and everything to try and explain why things are not exactly the way they want them. In their pique, these personalities lash out, and start making assumptions about the people around them. Those assumptions lead to accusations and cause far more trouble then these individuals are worth. In the end, it also shows another general lack of decency that is hard to stomach when you work so hard to be a better person and far better in acceptance than the generations that have come before.

Karen's are the proof that for every step forward humankind takes, we have regimes or naysayers who take four steps back to halt the progress and change before them. Which is why this subject is such a hot button, especially among people who work in the customer service industry.

So let us get down to the nitty gritty.

Karen's are not an easy subject to deal with, but I will do my best to stop at full on rant. That I can tell you, will not be an easy task.

The breakdown of the Karen starts with one simple word: entitlement.

These individuals truly believe that no matter the circumstance, the world owes them something. It is that belief that makes them feel the world, or at least the part of the world they live in, truly revolves around them singularly. This inflation of self and ego, causes them to move through situations in life as if they are the final and decisive word on everything. Forget the policies or rules of any establishment, if they wish to do something or acquire anything to their specification, it is to be theirs almost immediately. This is paramount to understand. A Karen will say that they are to get what they asked for, no matter the cost, the inconvenience, or the situation.

With that in mind, it is imperative that you understand such an individual will not fair well when they are told no. The minute anyone decides to stand their ground against a Karen, the situation will rapidly deteriorate. There is no way to avoid that unfortunate happenstance, but you can navigate it. Be aware, that the deterioration of the situation will have many possible incidents because a Karen does not limit their attacks and vitriol to one individual, but to anyone in the vicinity.

While this may seem far-reaching, personal accounts and situations with Karen's have allowed me to witness the following:
- Attacks against teenage workers trying to assist said Karen.
- Karen's verbally assaulting or screaming at autistic or mentally handicapped workers.
- Throwing food at employees in their work place.
- Money thrown at employees from moving vehicles at high speeds. (Change.)
- A customer jumping over a counter and punching a worker in the face.
- A customer spitting on counter surfaces and door handles then saying they were positive for COVID before storming out.
- An individual kicking a window and shattering it at a place of business.
- An individual trying to break down a Delivery Driver entrance door to force staff to take their order after closing time.
- Upending a drink/salad dressing/condiment onto a table and carpeted floor in protest of a store not having a particular menu item.

- Knocking over an arcade machine after being asked to leave a restaurant for being disruptive.

These are just in the food service industry. The amount of stories one can witness on videos in social media that outline a Karen's behavior in customer service areas or public view give a whole slew of other examples. It is truly a disgusting trend that needs to end.

When faced with a Karen in the customer service industry, you walk a fine line. There will be some situations you can deescalate quickly. Others, you will not be so fortunate. However, the way you approach these situations cannot deviate. There can be no room or margin for error.

When encountering a Karen, there can be no deviation from the script in dealing with a customer concern or complaint. No matter if you are aware they are lying, or choosing to ignore something they were told previously. Sad as it is to admit, more often then not, these scenarios occur because said Karen refuses to accept what they were told earlier, or something they chose to overlook. Admittedly, in some circumstances it will be due to human error, but in trying to fix it, you are in for a wild ride with the Karen personality.

Be warned, they will do their best to push your buttons to try and escalate the situation and cost YOU whatever your job is. The reasoning is, a new person means they can bully them into getting what they want. Sadly, that is how most Karen's approach scenarios.

Especially one dealing with policy or procedure you refuse to break or bend for them. That, my friends, is the rub. You have to maintain your standard and give no ground, while keeping yourself from being put in a scenario that costs you your job or possibly more. Make no mistake, a Karen will go so far as to call cops for any small thing to try and make you pay for denying them what they want.

The problem in these scenarios, is that the Karen personality always wants to be the exception to the rule. ALWAYS.

It does not matter if you tell them that what they are asking for is impossible of against policy, they will continue to push and twist to try and get what they want. Yes, in some circumstances it could seem easier to give them what they are asking for, but the cost at a later time will be detrimental. There is a reason certain things are against policy in the work place. If you make an exception for one, you will have to continue making that exception for them and anyone else who witnessed said scenario. Since companies weigh success on the bottom line of profit, and your actions are costing them money, you will be at fault. And once they rule that way, your days in that job are numbered.

So, in dealing with a Karen, no matter how enraged they are, you have to stand your ground. Doing so in the face of their opposition will be difficult to say the least.

Dealing with the Karen always begins the same, you maintain an even tone and work on being polite. Almost to a fault. The conversation will begin civil enough with the Karen making their demand or complaining about something that they wanted that they did not get to their standard of perfection. Now, this scenario could end quickly if it is a product of human error, at which point you can offer your apologies and have the order or item remade to replace the imperfection.

However, if it is something that is due to what they request being a breach in protocol or policy, the situation gets dicey. While you will begin with an apology, the situation will take a turn when you add in the part where you say that what they are asking for is not something you can accommodate. Whether that reason lies in the fact what they are asking for does not exist or breaks policy, does not matter. The minute you told them such a thing was not possible, the line has been drawn in the sand. So begins the altercation part of this encounter.

No matter how pleasant you have been, this will mean nothing when the Karen has been told no. So will begin the interrogation. It will not be gentle, and instead will be pointed and almost accusatory. The Karen in question will begin with the 'Why can't you give me what I want?' Your answer will make no difference. You can explain to great extent the what's and the why's, but there will be no understanding on the Karen's part. Whether you have explained to them in great detail the reasons or not, they will push further. Every single fact you give them will bring another question of why or what is causing them to not have what they want.

After this phase, will come the accusations. A Karen cannot fathom that they are being told that something is not possible, so they choose to believe that the person standing against them is doing so for nefarious purposes. Whether it's general dislike, or because of a certain factor that the Karen believes is in play, they will try and say that particular thing is why they are being denied what they want. While this is not, and in most scenarios is never true, it will not stop them from spewing it out. Karen's have been known to use race, age, religion, or even clothing as a factor for why someone would tell them no. Anything but the real reason, which is that what they want is against policy or not available for them to have. That answer does not exist in the world of the Karen.

You see, the world knows they are important, therefore what they want or ask for, is of the utmost importance. If you are to deny a Karen exactly what they ask for, you are impeding progress. More than that, you are being difficult and refusing to serve them because you have a problem with them in particular. This is the common story that Karen's spew about the people they are in a disagreement with. Sadly, this part of the altercation, while it is only the beginning, will seem to take forever. The Karen draws it out and continues to circle back to the same set of questions or explanations she was giving at the beginning. In this circumstance, the best that can be done is to remain absolutely calm. Do not show a hint of attitude and for the love of all that is holy, be sure to keep your voice monotone.

If there is even a hint of sarcasm in the words you speak, the altercation will escalate quickly. Make no mistake, the situation will escalate as it always does with a Karen in play, but it will happen faster if you have the misfortune of allowing your tone of voice to bleed with even a hint of sarcasm. Or, if you explain a policy for the umpteenth time and do so slowly and enunciate in an effort to try to get them to hear you. At that point, the Karen becomes rabid because they insist you are treating them like they are stupid.

With a Karen, it is a no win situation. Even if you do none of those things, when they get frustrated, the escalation to full blown tantrum begins. The next part of the altercation gets dicey. Karen will ask to speak to a manager, or someone higher up. Sadly if you're the person in charge, that's you. When they learn this particular fact, things will get even worse. However, if on this particular occasion your boss is there, they can be pulled in. Not that it will do any good. If the boss you have is the one who enforces the company policies, Karen is about to have the meltdown of all meltdowns when they get the exact same answers you gave. However, in either scenario what comes next is the main event.

Believe me when I say, Karen's do not register the world or people around them. Their own self-importance takes precedent. Whether it is yourself, or your boss, when it becomes clear to this personality that they are being told no, the full blown tantrum begins. While it does vary from Karen to Karen, the general consensus of how this takes place is the same. It is violent, rude, and disruptive much like the temper tantrums of a toddler learning how to navigate the world and being told no when they do something wrong.

It starts with screaming. Sometimes with cursing, sometimes not. When this part begins, your safest bet is to keep your voice neutral and passive. Gently remind them that while you understand their frustration what they are doing is not appropriate. Dependent on the Karen, some deflate at this point, however you're lifetime achievement Karen's will continue.

Those that do not back down, will then become increasingly aggressive. They will slam their hands on to counter, stomp their feet, point at other employees or customers and rage. More than once, one of these individuals have terrified other hapless customers. It is at this point you can assert yourself a little more. You can point out their behavior is disruptive and while you are sorry for their frustration, you think it would be best if they leave your establishment.

Will it work? Sometimes. If it does not make them see sense, you have to resign yourself to being in for a whole ride experience with said Karen. Sadly those only end one of three ways.

If the Karen refuses to leave, the next part is the one that puts you in jeopardy. The reason I say this is because the Karen is irrational and overly excited. Sometimes they just throw things randomly, whether it is whatever they can find nearest to them or they grab something from another customer or person to start launching it across the room, it can happen. Some Karen's even aim for other people. The whole time they are screaming and making threats, talking about how you steal from people or do not know how to treat your customers.

Sadly, if the Karen you are encountering is not an object thrower, they are the type that will lunge at you to do something physical. I have seen people with this personality try to grab employees and hold them still to scream at them. Shake someone as if they were trying to force them to wake up and see that they have to do what Karen asks to make the assault stop. I have seen Karen's that launch themselves behind service counters to begin slapping or punching employees. The utter list of ridiculousness continues, but the warning is the same. The Karen will use some sort of physical confrontation, whether by their own hand or flinging objects at others, depends on that particular individual.

The whole time this is taking place, they will be screaming and ranting. Talking about being judged and that you're stealing from them. They will begin demanding satisfaction and for the corporate number. Threats about making sure you know who you are dealing with and that they will have your job by the end of the day become abundant.

At this point, you can choose to get the police involved. Now, one thing that is particularly funny about this, is these Karen's will actually STICK AROUND for the cops to show up. Truthfully, they believe they are justified in their actions and that the cops will see what upstanding, awesome citizens they are and force the people they are arguing with to give them what they want. As much as it would seem that this is an exaggeration, it has been witnessed to often to count and each time the outcome remains the same. More often then not, if you even warn said Karen that you are calling the cops, they start screaming that you should. To get them there just as quickly as possible.

In the interim, said Karen will continue moving through your store or area like Godzilla through Tokyo. If it's not bolted down or secured, everything becomes a weapon and Karen will pick them up and launch them across the room. If it's not possible to do so, they will make as much of a mess as they can manage. One can hope this is where their rage is channeled, but sometimes it is focused on a person. The Karen will be aggressive and harming said person in some way, if that employee or target hasn't found a way to get free. If they had, the interim of time where you wait for law enforcement will be spent trying to pry the Karen off the employee or keeping her from getting to them, which again, puts yourself or others in the way of possible bodily harm.

Once the members of law enforcement arrive, it is sad to say the experience is not over. The first thing that will happen is officers separating you and your staff from the Karen. Then will begin the explanations. You will notice that upon the arrival of officer's Karen is once more docile. There is no belligerent ranting or screaming. If anything, your Karen will now act like she is the most innocent person on the planet. She will insist that you and your employees started the altercation.

It is imperative that you understand, you cannot lose your temper. No matter how badly you want to scream, talk over, or yell to make it clear that Karen caused the disturbance – you need to keep calm. Make no mistake, internally you will be raging, but showing it will not get you anywhere with solving the problem of the

Karen in your path. Rant later, for that moment, maintain as much of a calm as is possible. This more than anything else will help in your case.

Karen will spend her part of the explanation placing blame on any and everyone. This individual will tell the officers that they was merely trying to get what they paid for. The whole of the scenario will be turned around to try and make Karen look like the victim.

If one had been able to maintain their cool, by the time she is finished, when it is your turn to explain - officers will be more open to you. See, not many people realize it, but Karen's very much use the words, 'Me', 'I', and 'Mine'. That form of selfishness is not something that could be hidden. More than that, they tend to appear when a person is trying to justify their actions. Officers recognize this and more than that, others who witnessed Karen's episode can attest to it, if there isn't flat out video of the incident. The calmer you appear, the more forthright officers are in discerning the situation.

While Karen will earn her stripes, so to speak, you will be in the virtual clear.

Much as it galls me to have to even mention a Karen, let alone dedicate a whole chapter to them, it should be noted that this breakdown works even outside of the customer service industry. Admittedly, there are more resources to use in the public setting, such as recording the Karen on one's cell phone for evidence. Or using a business to seek shelter while said Karen is harassing you.

Do not be surprised at the lengths to which a Karen will go to make her point. The entitlement that these personalities have built up is extraordinary. They will accost anyone, stating the reasons they believe the act is justified. In the end, the best thing you can do is maintain your calm and not egg the Karen on. The faster that you can shut that down, the better. And that is where I will end this chapter, because I already feel like I have given the Karen way too much attention.

## CHAPTER 14
## LOONEY TUNES

One thing about the customer service industry that one can never escape, is music.

     Funny as it sounds, whether you are in food service, retail customer service, or just general telephone customer service there is always music involved. Sometimes in the weirdest ways imaginable. With that said, it also means that you will come into contact with some songs that will crawl on your absolute last nerve.

     Sometimes these songs will come to you courtesy of the company you work for. Other times it will be something you become privy to thanks to another employee. At other times, it will be something you encounter because of the customer themselves. The one thing all of these share in common is the fact that once exposed to that song, it will seem like it is impossible to get away from.

     Whether at work, or in our personal lives we have all joked about the infamous elevator music. These soft listening piano renditions of popular songs played at volume level four are enough to put anyone asleep. Yet, they would linger, sticking in our subconscious for days, perhaps even weeks afterwards. These little diddies are child's play.

Enter the world of customer service. From the nearest phone call center to the hallowed halls of your nearest big box store, the game has definitely changed. No longer is it the soft, sweeping piano melodies that pipe through the speakers at low volume. Oh, Nay.

Now, we are subjected to what people describe as oldies. Songs that we know from our own youth, or better yet, our parents youth. The songs that are slowly incorporating their way into the oldies radio genre are things we would prefer to stay dead and buried. Gems like 'MMmmm Bop' and 'Ray of Light' now permeate the airways in these stores. Reminding us of a time when we would search for the radio dial just to escape them the first time.

Sadly, there is no escape and its guaranteed if you are in said store for more than an hour, you will hear these songs at least twice. Much like their hey day, it will take weeks to get these songs out of your head after even hearing them once. To be forced to work an eight hour shift and hear these on repeat? Such an act is something that should be considered cruel and unusual punishment. While one can agree it would be nice to have music playing to ease the atmosphere of said store environment, there should be a ban on songs that are routinely found to be annoying or too repetitive. Sadly, that is not a choice anyone is given, whether they are a shopper or an employee.

While this is but one example of cringe worthy songs you could be forced to encounter, it pales in comparison to scenarios that you cannot extricate yourself from. The work place, is always an atmosphere that should be lightened. No matter the job, whether it be in an office, on the road, in your own home, or in a store - there are tasks and responsibilities that are monotonous for day to day life. Work in any environment comes with its own sets of stressors and difficulties. While it is necessary to do so and contribute to society as a whole, the repetitive nature of said work can become overbearing and hard to muddle through.

As such, any small thing to lighten up the work environment is helpful. In some cases, music is just the thing. Dependent on the job you work, that could change. In an environment with more than one employee present, there is no way everyone can listen to their personal music on their phones or electronics without it becoming an issue – other solutions have to be found. To be fair, if you have only six employees that are working in a small enclosed area and each one is playing their own music on their phone, it creates a cacophony of noise. Add to that, anyone trying to relay information or message from one employee to another will have to fight to be heard over the varying sounds filling the space.

Therefore, you find situations like this where more often then not, the leader or manager of that particular area will have a single speaker to generate music. Since they are the one leading that shift, they will typically choose the songs and make sure that whatever is playing is client/public friendly according to their company handbook. Sadly, not everyone listens to the same music. As such, this experience can be something immensely entertaining, semi-enjoyable, eye-opening, or finally just plain horrible.

Yes, tolerance is something we should all have. Sadly, one cannot dictate what and who controls the flow of music in a situation like this. At times it could seem daunting or even more frustrating, but every once in a while there is a small sliver of light and hope that accompanies these experiences. Whether it is discovering a new song or band that can be delved into later, or in finding relief when a new person takes charge of the listening device. Still, the music helps to break the monotony of the work day and give us at least one thing to focus on besides the pressures of work.

Still, there is no escaping the fact that these experiences, whether at work or home - help to expose us to things we would not normally come into contact with. As such, we also become subject to songs or melodies we would not encounter otherwise. From time to time, these occurrences bring us to certain tidbits that are better left forgotten. It never fails that even working amongst your peers, there will be one song that grates on someone's last nerve. When that happens, there is little that can be done. Yet, in the end, the knowledge of that music is now a real thing and with it, the realization that you are slowly learning that song as time passes on.

Just remember, it is only a song. You will not have to listen to it by choice anywhere else. It is a fleeting four minutes of your life, if you have to, hum under your breath to change the environment around you. While you may not be able to escape said tune, you can stop it from driving you to distraction. Especially if the dislike of said song is so deeply rooted that it makes you angry or impatient with the world at large. There is absolutely no reason to let these musical interludes push you to distraction.

Be you and push the music from your mind if it is in danger of sending you over the edge. In the end, try to be appreciative of having the music at all. If a problem persists, speak to your manager or the people around you to try and ask that alternative music be played. If that does not work in your favor, you can always hum to yourself to block out any unwanted sound or melodies that are to be avoided.

If possible, some work places will allow you to have in ear pods to listen to your own music. However, one should be mindful of the possibilities of using such a thing in public. People often believe that the use of air pods or ear phones is disrespectful to serving customer's in any environment, so this may not be the best method of compromise.

Just remember, nothing is permanent, not even the music playing, so either enjoy it as best you can and make jokes, or ignore it and wait for a time you can be more settled to enjoy what's playing. In the end, it is meant to be a help, not a hindrance. So do not let the existence of less than favorable tunes in your immediate area drive you looney. After all, you get to be your own DJ most of the rest of the time.

## CHAPTER 15
## MAKING THE GRADE

Well, this chapter is for food service employees and managers, period. Also, it will give all of you in the civilian walk of life a better idea of just what these inspections mean.

It has been discussed that my personal experience came from working at several food restaurant chains. While I do not underline where these experiences took place, there is one thing they all have in common. INSPECTIONS.

While more would say that an inspection should not be such a big deal, in all actuality it is what keeps a lot of these stores, bars, and restaurants open. So they are in fact, a very big deal, no matter how small or short-timed these visits are. It also does not matter what type of inspection it is, the minute that the person doing the inspection walks in the door, the stress of the work place increases ten fold. The worst part is knowing, you will be docked points for things beyond your control.

So, let us begin the nerve wracking quest of inspections with one that people like to rip apart even in public venues – the Health Department Inspection. Yes, I am aware that these are intended to give people an idea of the cleanliness of the restaurant they are eating in. Allow me to tell you, 'Surprise!' the Health

Inspection is not at all what you think it is. While yes, I will stipulate that the cleaner the store the higher the number, however, even a mega-clean store can get a score as low as a ninety-two over things not in their control. For instance – it has been witnessed that two separate locations that were immaculate inside and had perfect food safety practices got scores as low as a ninety based on conditions not in the restaurant's direct control.

In these cases, it dealt with dumpsters that were a good thirty feet away from the building itself. The dumpster's did not have doors to close them off from the public. More so, they had not been replaced by the refuse company in more than fifteen years. The concrete that the dumpster's sat on, was broken and cracked, stained from years of use. The drain plugs on the dumpsters were long gone as they had broken or cracked due to being out in the elements. The restaurant itself had no control over these aspects as the trash receptacles were owned and controlled by the refuse company. Yet, the restaurant lost points for all of this. More than that, the fact the dumpsters could not be replaced while the official from the health department was there, docked them another two points.

Yet another store lost points on an inspection because an employee grabbed a towel to wipe down the heat rack where food is held. Literally cleaning the store in front of the inspector. When they were done, they placed the rag on a counter top nearby because they had used a certain cleaner on it. The Health Inspector then docked them three points because the rag was not in sanitizer. Mind you, if the rage had been placed in sanitizer, the chemical on it would have spread to the rags actually being used on food contact surfaces, thereby contaminating them. Still, they lost points for doing what most would consider the right thing in preventing cross-contamination. All because according to them, any rag that is used in store, should immediately be dropped in sanitizer when it's over.

Again, wrong focus. Yet, lowering the health department's overall score for the restaurant to make them appear as a risk. When in fact, they are probably cleaner than most hospitals. A fact I can say given my experience in working in both fields. The amount of small things the Health Department tries to use to affect the score, that are tantamount to idiocy is mind boggling. Especially when they do not impact the restaurant interior.

Yet, these changes will never be made and the staff who work for way less money then people in other lines of work, are left to scramble and fix said problems on their own. The worst part is, very few people realize just how much has to be done in order to make these places clean and healthy, while following the standards for proper food handling. More than that, even with these responsibilities, people decry those working in food service and tell them to get real jobs. As if doing things within standard and stopping hundreds of people from getting sick from eating food prepared by others isn't a real job. Or keeping things safe for their customers who have allergies, or even separating foods to avoid cross contamination. Still, no one thinks of these things when they are talking of food service jobs, but I digress. We are instead talking about making the grade for inspections and we shall now return to it.

Now that we have addressed the Health Department Inspection we can move on to the others. Part of what makes restaurant work so daunting is that there is always more than one kind of inspection to be ready for. It is why, the importance of food safety, correct products, expiration dates, and food preparation to standards are so important. Especially in the chain restaurant business. While the general public may not be aware, anyone who works in the food industry in a restaurant chain not only has to meet and comply with local inspections from the Health Department, but a corporate inspection from the head honchos as well.

These inspection happen at least twice a year, and sometimes dependent on the store, the amount of business, or noted complaints of a certain type, can happen more than that. As thorough as the public believes the Health Department can be, it's these corporate inspections that get down to the nitty gritty. Everything the Health Department takes a look at is included in these corporate inspections, however they are added, more intricate details applied. These corporations want their product to be consistent no matter where the store in question is located. So these inspections require the staff to show that not only do they use safe food practices, but do so while maintain the preparation and standards of the company as a whole.

This requires an inspection that goes beyond that of the Health Department. While they check most of the same things such as holding temps, storage temperatures, hand washing stations, ect. - they also break the whole store down to take a closer look at the smallest of things. They look at air vents for dust, baseboards around the store for any kind of deviation from their shape or display, walls, functional paper towel and soap dispensers. That is just the beginning.

When you move to food safety it is a whole new nightmare. Where before you just had to worry about temperatures, dates, and controlling those factors – now it becomes something much more complicated. These inspections require you to show the whole process of how you handle your food. From the temperatures they are kept in, to the system you use for preparation. It is a time consuming task, not only that, but even as you are doing this, you have to try and make sure that those left to run your store are doing everything correctly. True, you should be doing this all the time, but if you have a new employee or someone who is being trained in certain aspects but not others because of timing, it can get dicey. When you are also the manager who should be teaching these employees, you cannot be there to guide them and teach them properly.

While these inspections serve their purpose, they also set you up for failure in some ways. However, most stores are quick to implement correct training if they are committed to the standards of the store. Sadly, even the most committed of these managers will never be able to cover everything. That said, the detail of these inspections is so intricate that one has no choice but to move with the inspectors through the store to be sure to explain or answer the questions that are posed. In some cases, to show actual proof of the practices that the manager has put in place to be sure they meet the guidelines set by corporate.

When it comes to product, the inspection gets even more difficult. Many people do not realize that the food seen on television commercials is typically crafted out of building materials and painted to look perfect. This places a burden on anyone who works in food service to try and create such perfection with the actual ingredients in store. Perfection is not easy to accomplish, especially with differentiating factors that one will run into. No oven will run exactly the same between stores. The air quality will always be different. The water density and chemicals will be different, as will the minerals present in such things.

Factors will always influence the outcome. So when a corporate inspection is taking place, you never know what it will entail. There is no way to predict just what kind of food will be ordered when the inspector is there, but one thing is certain. You will be trying to make that food appear as perfect as possible. For most of these inspections, they will judge and grade the products that come out of the oven for a good amount of time. Is it cooked too long? Does it lack the right amount of toppings? Is the customer getting what they paid for? Was it prepared exactly the way it should have been?

Each step of the process is taken into consideration. Even the final result is broken down into differentiating criteria. The first being temperature upon completion. This is also where the most things in the inspection can go wrong. Considering most companies outline their recipes through weights or count measures, they are extremely picky on the presentation of the food. Almost all of them will count every single topping on the food to be sure the guidelines are being followed to the letter.

The worst part, is that as hard as these inspections are to pass, they also have the potential to rip your job from underneath you. Corporate inspection that fail, for whatever reason, can put you on a watch list or have your store shut down completely. There is no in-between.

Once an inspection like this had been failed, one cannot hope for a form of limbo to buy time to correct the mistakes. The answer to come is swift, decisive, and without measure. More than once, General Managers have gone to work and been met with people from the corporate level that escort them off the premises and issue in a new person to take the fired manager's place.

All of these inspections are things you have to be ready for at the drop of a hat. All day, every day. Yet, people still decry anyone who works in the service industry, saying they should find a real job. While they are under fire with such claims, they are also working to be as perfect as possible to pass these inspections so that no one in the store is subject to more ridicule for a low score, or a loss of points.

Juggling such things is not easy, to say the least. So the next time you look at a score for any particular restaurant or even a store, think of all the work that goes into garnering those awards. Some places encourage their customers to ask why their scores are what they are. You would be surprised at some of the answers. So with that said, keep in mind, these employees are not just working to satisfy you, the customer. They are also striving for excellence among the general public, other restaurants or stores of a similar nature, and their bosses. Unlike those in many other fields, they have to be ready to be inspected at a moment's notice with no forewarning. That in itself, speaks volumes.

## CHAPTER 16
## NEGATIVE NANCY

There is always that one person that we encounter who always sees the world as a decimating event. The glass for them is always half empty with no chance of being refilled.

It is only fair that I acknowledge this personality openly. That's right, the personality in question, or rather under the spotlight, is the Negative Nancy.

Whether it is in the store, on the phone, or in our everyday lives at home or work, there is at least one individual who fits this persona. The Negative Nancy is not to be taken lightly. Their pessimistic view of the world and generally annoyed temperament, is something that influences and affects all those around them.

While normally this persona is benign, in customer service it is detrimental when the individual embodying said personality is in a mood. All it takes is one muttered word or sarcastic comment to light the match for general unrest among staff or customers. Sadly, if and when this happens it can result in a domino effect that leaves you scrambling no matter what side of the fence you are on.

When you are working in the service industry and encounter a customer like this, it can be a trial to keep the situation contained. As a Negative Nancy is already a malcontent on the whole, when they are irritated or annoyed with an item or dish from a restaurant, these individuals can get boisterous in making their displeasure known. Typically, it starts with a generalize comment that you have one chance to answer.

Most often, this comment is along the lines of 'So I take it you are out of this [object] and will not have any more in until the next shipment?' To be fair, in some scenarios, you will have to tell them that said object or item is currently unavailable, but being able to tell them when the next shipment will be in, can diffuse the situation quickly. There will still be a few woe is me comments like, 'well it figures the one day I can make it here, the thing I want is not here' or 'I suppose I'll just try again next time, not like it will be any different then, either.' Regretfully, these comments, if overheard can sometimes start the murmur of discord among other customers.

Additionally, these comments can be made when a Negative Nancy is told that a particular food item or additional instruction for their meal, cannot be fulfilled. Unlike the Karen, the Negative Nancy will not blame you, per se – but the will bemoan their fate in not having what they want available to them. Funnily enough, everyone else will take it the other way and beginning to voice their annoyances and concerns without impunity. This is a domino effect and sadly only the first domino has to fall in order to make all the others cascade around you like a ton of bricks.

When these complaints begin, their will be a murmur, a pulse of energy that rouses the customers before you and makes them more agitated. Suddenly, tempers are shorter, attention spans more worn thin, and people less understanding of simple mistakes or the like. It is not the Negative Nancy themselves that will make your life or job difficult, it is the people they influence around you.

However, in some cases you can head off a Negative Nancy at the pass. There is a way to salvage the situation as long as you are willing to listen. Most times, these personalities are just seeking some form of reassurance or even a small light of hope at the end of the monotonous tunnel they travel everyday. Techniques to do such a thing are extremely simple and less time consuming than one might imagine.

In the case of a customer that embodies this archetype, be sincere. Apologize for the inconvenience and try to find something similar or that very object to relate to the customer with. If they are looking for a specific type of pen, or even marker, mention you understand how important that is or that you too favor that particular type of pen or object. If possible, give them a date as to when you may be back in supply of said object or utensil, and apologize again for not having in readily available.

Unlike the Karen, most Negative Nancy's will not be confrontational. A little perturbed and possibly a lot barky, they normally acknowledge you in kind and give a grudging thanks. While they may still carry their 'woe is me' attitude, they are far less likely to be muttering or cursing under their breath to get some kind of confrontation started. While it is not an outright shift in attitude, it goes a long way to stop them from riling up other customers with their sentiments.

That is the danger of the Negative Nancy. If you cannot control their comments, or their musings, it can spread to other customers in the surrounding area. If this happens you are in for a long litany of complaints for however long those people are present. Think of it like a virus. It starts in one specific cell or body, and then is spread to another cell. It rapidly begins to multiply and overwhelm the one dealing with it. The Negative Nancy attitude is the same.

Unlike a Karen, the Negative Nancy, despite their pessimism, is a generally likable person. Not just by you, but by other customers. This is why their malcontent seems to spark an answering emotion in others. Where the Karen is abrasive and rude, the Negative Nancy is relatable. Not kicking up a huge fuss, but generally upset by the lack of the item or object they want. It echoes in the sentiments of those around them to create a domino effect and bring other people into the picture to also feel such malcontent personally.

The best you can do with these situations is try and be as accommodating and apologetic as possible. While it will not be done easily, it can for the most part be salvaged. Just remember, to these personalities, whatever they are fixating on is important. Treat it that way. Once you do that, the situation will start to resolve itself, at least as much as it can be for that specific time.

## CHAPTER 17
## ONE FOR THE MONEY...

Whether you are an employee, a manager, or a customer there is one thing everyone is focused on...money. As such, people will save every penny they can to get the bigger, better deal. Which brings us to talking about a topic that can cause more disruptions in the service industry than any other...coupons.

While these seem benign enough you can be assured it is not. For anyone in retail or food service, coupons comprise about seventy percent of the work day. People looking for the best deals on the shelves, or asking about specials that one may find in the store that day. The issue with this is the loopholes that are given to staff and managers alike by companies. Sometimes the better deals, are not ones you can just give out and apply. Other coupons are limited to certain parameters and customers are displeased in learning they can't have exactly what they want, right now.

It is this particular point, that makes coupons such an argument. One that will likely remain as long as we function as a society. So rest assured, when the zombie outbreak occurs coupons will be a monster of the past, but until then we will be seeing them make an appearance often.

Now, it is important to understand the dynamics that have made coupons such a big deal. Coupons may seem benign enough, but when one factors in the other mitigating events that make these coupons important it puts the customer and the employee on opposite sides of the line. The reason for this is simple. Money.

The cost of living has continued to increase by leaps and bounds for the last thirty years. Along the way, we have adapted, spouting various ways to give discounts that keep businesses in mind and relevant. Coupons and deals have become the mainstream way that these businesses draw people in and keep them as customers. It is an age old trick that is being reinvented in new and interesting ways daily thanks to the internet. As society went more mainstream and tech became a thing, the way these stores offered themselves up became more integrated. Shopping programs that allowed you to shop specific deals, earn points, or even cash back became new ways of saving money.

As one would expect, we focused on trying to get the most bang from our buck. The bigger, better deals waiting around every corner. Coupons no longer got printed in the Sunday paper, but instead sent in emails online. Through it all, companies then began building apps and websites to order their services and the trend continued.

Now, we have apps upon apps, all proclaiming new discounts and new coupons.

Even stores that had once been considered big, box bargain stores, now have their own programs to try and force us to pay to get better discounts and service. Through it all, we continue to pinch and save, looking for the smallest ways to eliminate the price and cost of the items we are trying to acquire. Which brings us to now.

Most days, people do not even stop to think about the fact that most businesses are going mainstream with online ordering. With that in mind, they also know doing such things to encourage others to order on these websites or apps is in their best interest. As such, few people realize that the companies shifted their focus, and that the "specialty" deals one could get in store were becoming fewer and far between. This is most prevalent in food service.

It is important that people understand, not all the deals one finds online can be gotten in stores. Many companies have denied their in-store personnel the ability to give these deals in order to entice their customers to use their website and app for ordering. With that, there comes a divide when customers are dealing with over the phone orders and the employees in-store. More than that, companies also are seeking to encourage the public to spend more money so the specials that one is offered on the phone will never be the same as the low-priced money savers people will find online.

An example of this is best found among the food service industry dealing with chain pizza businesses. Almost every single franchise offers a coupon for a large pizza with one to three toppings for $7.99. For those looking for more than one pie, there is a coupon titled the meal deal or mix and match where you get smaller pizzas with one topping, etc. for $6.00 each. Now, these are lucrative and money saving deals for some people, and the public will fall back on these two if they fail to find something else they want. However, here comes the rub...

Neither of these coupons is readily available in store. One, will be an online only exclusive, while the other coupon is one that a customer will have to ask for. All joking aside, it is drilled into these employees that they never just apply a coupon to an order. The company is all about making that dollar more, and to do so, you are told that you only apply a coupon if a customer asks for it.

This is also why I tell everyone to be patient with the people taking your order. On more than one occasion, it has been witnessed that a customer in their rush to be heard, completely skips over the employee greeting and starts right to the order. Once they get told the total, they go ballistic because they are given the amount based on what they ordered. Then after all is said and done and the food paid for, they ask what specials are available. This song and dance will continue and then they will says that the last time they ordered the exact same thing they only paid a certain amount.

More often then not, this conversation ends poorly because many customers do not like being told that they have to ask for the coupon they want since it will not be automatically applied. That reaction is worse if they are told that the discount or coupon they wish to use can only be found online. Many a confrontation had happened in the last several years with people being told that these policies are in place. Worse, the aging population that does not wish to use or learn to use apps or internet ordering make it a fight when they argue with employees at the register. They want the coupon they saw advertised and being told that is an impossibility makes them generally rude and cantankerous to put it mildly.

While yes, coupons are good to advertise one's business. They are causing their fair share of problems as well. Few people will ever realize just how horrendous such an encounter is until they witness it for themselves. Sadly, there will be some customers you just cannot make happy. There are those that will not understand being told 'no' whether it is by the companies standards or your own. It is important to remember that while this is not something under your control per se, you still have to be able to explain it to the customer in such a way that does not seem condescending or rude.

It needs to be addressed that there is no point in getting frustrated with the workers. They will tell you that the coupon you are asking for is online only. When they tell you that they cannot offer you that same price in store, it is not an exaggeration. These stores are not given any kind of coupon code, to apply to an order to give you the same price. They can offer you any of the in store specials, which will always be the four main coupons that the company is willing to promote. But not the coupons for the large for way cheap or anything that says online only.

The mix-up/meal deal coupons that advertise pizzas for multiple pies cheap is one that you have to ask for. To be precise, these coupons are a huge discount that pretty much knock the price of the pizza down to cost. As such, they will not be something that the staff automatically offer to anyone. If you ask for a medium pizza, they will charge you full price unless you ask for that deal specifically. Again, these workers are trained to sell you food for the maximum dollar, as such, any coupon that discounts food at a huge price will be one you specifically have to ask for.

When you call stores, no matter the brand or location, the specials that they will recite to you that are available in that particular store will be a discount of sorts. Just not necessarily one that gives you more bang for your buck. Sadly with the accessibility of online ordering, most of your better deals will only be found there as more and more companies are working to streamline their products. Do not be surprised if you find that some coupons or discounts you see online for any store or website, is not something readily available in stores. In the case of retail, be aware you may have to have the scan code for those discounts readily available on a phone or electronic device in order to have it applied.

  The devil will always be in the details. Sad to say, but there is little you can do to change that. Also, be aware that with the advancement of technology a lot of things will only be accessed online since most businesses are leaning towards that infrastructure. In the end, be prepared for the changes that come with that whether you are the customer or an employee.

  These shifts in business can create a headache. As long as you are prepared for the situation, everything should resolve itself. That said, you will always have exceptions to this. People who refuse to use the apps or website and as such will be complaining to you that they are not able to access that deal. The best you can do is offer them the better deal among the ones you have readily available. If that does not work, there is no shame in apologizing and telling the customer point blank that you do not have access to what they are asking for. True, they may not believe you, but better that and explaining it to your manager's than to try and circumvent said rule and finding yourself in jeopardy of losing your job.

## CHAPTER 18
## PIOUS PETE

There are few things worse in life than a Karen. However, there is one that takes the cake. This personality is the Pious Pete. They are without a doubt the worst example of humanity to date. The reason that they oust Karen from the position is these people wrap up their prejudices, short comings, and attacks in the guise of righteous fervor because of their position or membership in a certain church or organization.

Note, I said church or organization because it is not just religious zealots that can be Pious Pete's. A person associated with a certain business or social group can be just as righteous in their views to justify their inexcusable behavior. It is no different when you are dealing with them in the service industry. However, it pales in comparison to those who use religion as their justification.

While that is not to say they are not as bothersome, it is easier to stomach radical members of a group without religious affiliation. Those who hide behind their beliefs, especially Christianity, have the ability to make someone choke on their own bile.

The problem with these particular people, is they will smile to your face and accept your politeness. On the surface, they seem completely and totally understanding of any apology or situation. Then, the moment you turn your back, they become the very creature they denounce with their belief. As horrific as this sounds, those that boast of being the most devout of believers, will turn out to be the most judgmental and deceitful customers you will ever have to deal with.

Make no mistake, believe as you will. Too each their own. If religion makes you happy, than by all means, follow that path. However, keep to the precepts of your chosen faith. The example used for the Pious Pete will be one that is common here in the south eastern United States. As many will be aware, these states are referred to openly as the bible belt. This is done with good reason.

A majority of the population in these states, claim to be Christian. Ranging from Southern Baptist to Free Will Non-Denominational, most citizens of these states proclaim some tie to that particular belief system. The reason that their behavior is something to be found galling, is that at its core, the Christian religion speaks of being better to your fellow man. To showing compassion, love, gratitude, and moral standing as a shining example of their belief in following God and his son.

The actions witnessed by these same people is a sickening opposite that they subject the world to. More than that, twisting the words of their own faith to justify their own selfish needs or ridiculous demands. Worse, some use that faith to justify their hostilities and hatred towards others.

Most often when you encounter the Pious Pete, they will smile to your face. When you tell them the issue, or apologize, they will nod and smile, nod their head and say they understand. However, from that point, they will begin to castigate or complain about the problem. Some will step up and ask if you know who they are, then describe in detail the position within the church of their choice. Then, will begin the soliloquy on how they would have handled just such a situation among their parish or family. All of it is nothing more than double sided speak to accuse the staff before them of incompetence.

After this, comes the judgment on the staff in general. Some will even go so far as to say that the ones choosing to be at work are doing the devil's work. Choosing money over a fruitful and enriched life walking with the Lord. You may laugh, but the sad truth is these things have actually happened.

The irony of this is, they are the reason such people have to work. They go to their church services and on release move to find places to eat, drink, and fellowship together. Sadly, that fellowship does not include kindness to their fellow man. These Pious Pete's will sit at their table in judgment of everyone around them. Other customers and their manner of dress, the actions of the staff as they try to hurry from table to table to satisfy multiple customers, even the behavior of children that are in the general vicinity.

What is disturbing about these individuals is the complete hypocrisy of their actions in relation to the religion they practice. A belief system built on love, peace, harmony, acceptance, gentleness, and kindness being wielded like a weapon against people who are doing their best to provide food services for others. Yet, they will continue to lie, cheat, steal, yell, and destroy any and everyone in their path to get what they want. They will spew insults and hatred in order to try and affect a change to their order or food, whether it is appropriate or not. There is nothing too far, no action too demanding for them to attempt to gain what they want from these types of encounters.

In dealing with the Pious Pete's of the world, no matter their religion of choice, your method of dealing with them will remain the same. Whether you are a customer, an employee, a service worker, or just an everyday joe who encounters one of these individuals – the solution remains the same.

Kill them with kindness.

Something that has infested the world of religion is the idea of status. Their reputation among their peers must be without blemish. As such, when you become the epitome of what they should embody in their own religion, you force them to step back.

Being polite, generally pleasant, and in the case of a service worker, penitent for the mistake with their order or item. Doing these things with a cool, no nonsense attitude, especially among their peers will garner you great progress in resolving the issue faster. More than that, it could diffuse the situation where they were complaining since they must show some form of benevolence in the face of your soft spoken and heartfelt apology.

Be mindful, meeting a Pious Pete with anger, will escalate the situation. In most cases, it will only be a verbal altercation, but I can promise you, it will be very impassioned. Try to avoid this at all costs, because if the Pious Pete gets riled, they will be zealous in their defense. So, always remember, kindness before all in these situations.

# CHAPTER 19
# QUALITY CONTROL

One of the worst things to have to keep in mind as both customer and employee in the service industry in quality control. Believe it or not, this is something even the customer thinks about, although to them it is seen in other terms or phrases, but in the end, it is the same thing.

This characteristic is most prevalent in food service. Customers want what they paid for, and will be able to spot the difference in their food quickly. That is why so many restaurants have standards that should be measured and gone by. On the service side of things, quality control is key to making sure that you maintain the standards that customers have come to expect of your company. More than that, making sure the food is as close to perfect as possible ensures that your customer is pleased with their purchase and enjoys the food.

In truth, when people pay for food, they should be getting flavor and enjoyment, not grease and disappointment. Well, for the most part. Sadly I can say, that if you are getting fast food, most of that is pure grease, but you certainly don't want to order something like a big mac, and have burger patties you can't see on the bun. It's about making sure you give the customer what they want and ask for. Period.

Now admittedly, in some cases these are impossible to maintain. I reference the earlier chapter where we discussed a pizza that had cheese on one half, but no cheese on the other. There is absolutely no way to fulfill that request because with sauce involved, when the cheese melts, it will bleed over to the non cheese side of the pizza. Sadly, physics is not planning to play nice in this little game of happenstance. However, on the other side of things when the customer orders straight from the menu, you should be doing everything in your power to make sure they get exactly what they ask for as close to perfection as possible.

This can be a rather difficult thing to do, but not impossible. The hardest part about quality control is making good food and not blowing portions to do it. This is a fine line to walk in some areas, especially dependent upon the supplies that you have to work with. That is something that is not always within your control. It also serves to make life harder some days.

For example, let us choose a topping to illustrate the point. So let's say you order from a supply company, who in turn, contracts to get certain food items from different vendors. So, to fulfill the demand of that particular supply, they contract one to three different places to fulfill their demand. Now, that hub gets an order from a hub or restaurant and begin shipping those products out to these smaller businesses. So, now you are getting this one product from several different sources, and as orders come in, you pull from one stock pile to send out and two days later, use a completely new one to send out the same supply.

So now, we move on to how this impacts you. Let's use a topping that illustrates this point well.

Bacon. Why? Because most people love bacon, even if they do not eat it, because that is a smell unparalleled with any other. However, for any vegans who may be reading this, I do apologize.

So, you are in your store, sending off for your truck. You notice you are low on bacon and order a case. That case arrives two days later and you get these perfectly marbled pieces of bacon that are big enough to spread on a pizza visibly. It is lean, with only small amounts of fat and when it cooks up, it is crispy and gives a nice smoked saltiness. This gains notice and you sell a few more pizzas than normal with bacon on it. Now, with supply increasing you place an order for another supply truck with a new case of bacon on board.

This time, when your order is received, the lot of bacon you got before has been depleted. When the supply company sends you this order the bacon that is delivered is mostly fat. This bacon creates a lot of grease as it cooks and the fat burns off, causing the bacon to shrink to small, speck like amalgams that resemble burned crumbs and in turn make your customers angry. There is little you can do to change the bacon, but you still have to make the customer happy. Sometimes the only way to do that is to offer to remake the pizza with a different topping, or another item altogether.

As stated earlier, sometimes the quality issues are out of your control. Others, however, are completely within your purview. While yes, you can only do so much, when you're in food service you can check every single part of an order to be sure it meets the standard you want for your customers. Happy customers means booming business. Booming business means people returning for more and referring you to others. One thing inevitably feeds the other.

That model of business, that need for sustainable income, is also tempered by the operating cost. You have to be able to provide good service while not blowing the bank. Part of that, exists in quality checking all orders. In some scenarios the fix is an easy one, like a pepperoni pizza that the customer requests have no garlic seasoning on the crust. When it comes out of the oven, and you make the mistake of putting garlic seasoning on, the situation can be rectified by switching the pizza out with the next pepperoni coming out of the oven and leaving off the garlic seasoning.

Sometimes, quality control means seeing an order is wrong, and refusing to send it out to the customer that way. As monotonous and time consuming as quality control may be in your particular line of work, in the end it will save you more time and money then if you send out mistakes and have to correct them later. It is time consuming, it will also cause your employees or coworkers a great deal of stress in replacing said items, but the customer will be happy. The added bonus of being so vigilant in quality control this way, is that it will cut down on the same mistakes being made in the future, allow you to control your inventory a lot better, and set you up to stream line operations so that these incidents will become few and far between.

  Sadly, while you institute these kinds of standards, there will be a lot of frustrations and grumbling. Not just from your coworkers and staff, but your customers alike. That will pale in comparison to your own internal frustrations and grumblings while you enforce said standards.

  As a customer, you will find these moments tedious. However, these situations can become advantageous for you if you show gracefulness in the process. For instance, if you were to order a pizza and something comes out wrong when they pull it from the oven. If a store is trying to raise standard and calls for a remake for the mistake, or even something going wrong like the dough sticking to the screen, you can benefit. Most restaurants will apologize for such a wait, offer you a free drink or a dessert of some sort for the trouble. Some will even offer you the messed up pizza in addition to what you actually ordered, or a discount in the future. This varies from manager to manager and company to company depending on their procedures for customer satisfaction. It can be said that your reaction will guide theirs. If you are short, curt, or rude over the problem, most will only offer the bare minimum to keep you happy.

However, if you can be gracious, there is no limit to the amount of things this staff will do to keep you happy. They will thank you and offer you any and everything they can for being so understanding. Always remember, even as a customer, the adage 'you attract more flies with honey' is very true. We are all human, when that is something people recognize, it makes the whole world breathe a little easier.

That said, also take note they call for this remake so you get EXACTLY what you want. Quality control, while somewhat tedious, is intended to be sure that you acquire all that you want and get your money's worth. It is a benefit to both you and the company you are dealing with.

With all that said, I believe that this is a good place to finish this subject. There is little else that can be said or done to clarify the importance of this issue and why one should stick to it. In the end, the benefit is for both sides and should be a practice addressed everywhere.

# CHAPTER 20
# ROBBERY PROTOCOLS AND OTHER WAYS TO SURVIVE

Now, we will touch on a subject that all retail/food service workers fear. One thing they do not consider is that it is a fear of their customers as well. Robbery is a very real thing in these industries and as such is something that everyone on staff should be trained for.

  However, no one mentions the customers. Despite several jobs spanning over different companies, the training videos for these situations always mentions what you should do for yourself and your staff to make it through a robbery. There has never been one video that has mentioned what to do with or for your customers. Unfortunately, that is where we encounter a lot of issues when these situations happen.

  This needs to be very clear, to everyone. Employee, customer, passers-by, managers: There is no place in a robbery situation for heroes. No matter your intention, no matter if you are an off-duty police officer that is trained for high stress, violent situations – in this setting there is no place for people who want to save the day. The reason I say this is because of the training that employees who work in retail or food service receive on these scenarios.

It is important to understand that anyone faced with a robbery scenario, is in the position of dealing with said robber because the person committing the crime is desperate. Desperate people will do desperate things because they believe there is no other way out. This makes them all the more likely to lash out and harm others to accomplish whatever their goal might be. It is this rationale, that guides the policy of most every store in their robbery procedures and protocols. This is also the reason why employees who take risks in stopping thefts, gunmen, or robbery situations are typically removed from those companies in question.

The running policy for any of the above situations is simple. You are to give the robber anything he wants. Avoid looking at them directly, do your best to comply with their demands as quickly and efficiently as possible. Do not communicate threats or be confrontational. The instructional videos are very clear in the fact they want you and your co-workers to pay attention, but to cede all control to the robber.

These instructions make the procedure very clear. Not once should you try to intervene personally to stop the robbery. No confrontation of any type should take place with the robber. Give them what they want, as quickly as possible. Make them aware if other employees or persons will be coming in to the store, so they realize you're being honest and there is a clock on the amount of time they have. Follow the robber's instructions and do your best to keep him from wildly moving his attention around the room.

The reason it is important for everyone to understand what people are taught in these robbery and prevention videos is so they act accordingly in the situation should it ever occur. More than that, if people in the general public are aware of these protocols, they can avoid doing anything to interject themselves in the situation and make it escalate so someone is harmed. Many people, have a misguided belief that if a robbery or pick-pocketing were to happen in a retail or food service store, the staff should intervene.

That belief is a falsehood that many should be made aware of. Any employee of any company that serves the public, is trained in the same way. To be non-confrontational and make the situation move as flawlessly as possible to facilitate the safety of all involved. It is this reason, that most news stories one reads about an employee being fired after detaining a purse snatcher or thief becomes news. No one can wrap their head around the fact that while yes, the employee recovered the money or objects stolen, had their gamble been wrong, it could have resulted in the injury or even death, or other employees or customers.

The training provided on these situations is abundantly clear, we are not law enforcement. We are not superheroes. It is our job to give the robber what they ask for and do so as quickly and quietly as we are able to be sure they move along quickly. Giving in to their demands, following their instructions and giving them the money or product they ask for is the easiest way to resolve the situation with no one getting hurt.

That said, it is important that anyone who finds themselves in a robbery situation whether at work or out and about, realize that there is no medal for someone who dies trying to stop the act. While we all decry the need for heroes in these situations and fantasize over the men in movies that put a wrench in the plans of criminals - the reality is that there is no place for people like this in the real world. There is no dress scene. No do over. If these situations go wrong, very real individuals lose their lives.

Reality, will never be as accepting or as well timed as movies. There will never be that moment of perfection to foil the robbery plot without some very serious consequences to the person intervening or others around them. That is the sad fact of the matter.

With that in mind it is important that you understand the training these customer service workers undergo. That way, you know that in such a situation, following their lead and getting as much space between you and the robber is best. Keep out of their focus, do not make sudden movements or approach them. Let the incident play out to the robber's discretion to make the situation as safe as possible for all involved.

That said, not all robberies happen in the stores. In the case of food service, there is a chance that any store that runs a delivery service will have some kind of robbery issue. That is not to include generalized money scams, but we will touch on that a bit later.

In recent years, we have seen an uptick of violent crimes against delivery individuals. Whether they work in food service or for the post office or even Amazon, the very real threat remains of having something stolen from you while you work. There have been numerous reports of stolen orders, items, even delivery vehicles.

With this in mind, customers also seem to forget that these are hazards. On more than one occasion there have been complaints because deliveries were not received, or flat out brought back to the stores they came from due to questionable environments. Many do not understand the reasons that these things happen. It should be noted, most do not consider the picture that gets painted by their house to others in the world. In order to clear up some of this, there are some simple steps you can take to avoid these incidents of undeliverable or returned orders due to sketchy settings.

**Always have your porch light on.** Most instructional videos for any kind of delivery service states that you should not get out of your car if you cannot see. A well lit area, makes it far easier to read numbers on mailboxes or houses, as well as make a person aware of their environment. Considering the very real possibility of being robbed, having a house that is well lit and ready to receive a visitor makes it more inviting to the person delivering your order.

**Make sure you have the numbers for your address clearly displayed.** I cannot stress this enough. More often then not, a returned delivery that is considered suspect because the address 'doesn't exist' is due to the driver not being able to see the numbers on the house or mailbox. It should also be noted, that robbery prevention videos clearly state that one should not exit their vehicle if they are in question of the address that they are delivering to. Keep in mind, most prank orders where a false address is given, end as robberies that can result in the driver being assaulted or even killed. So these guidelines can be lifesaving to the worker that is delivering your food.

**Answer your phone!** I cannot stress this point enough. When a driver is in doubt, especially in food delivery, they will call the number that is listed on your order. More than that, your phone number allows these companies to keep track of your orders so that they can correct an issue if your order is wrong.

That said, when you order a delivery and the driver is having a difficult time finding your residence, they are limited on options.

    The first is to take the food back to the store and wait for you to call back. While this is an option it is one that is frustrating to you, the customer - and the staff of the store in question. Taking an order back to the store, means you either get cool food when it goes back out for the second time and you're still upset you had to wait. Or you have an order that is freshly remade, which you can't appreciate because your irritated at the wait. Not to mention, the staff who had to remake the order because it did not reach its destination the first time. A situation that could have been avoided if someone had just chosen to answer their phone when the driver or store they ordered from called.

    The second option is to find what they think is the address since they cannot reach you and try to deliver the food. This can end one of three ways. The first is that it is your address and the problem is resolved. The second, is that it is the wrong address and the person there chooses to take your food, and either pays for it, or gets it for free because you already paid with a card. In this scenario, there is no way to verify that the person they are speaking to is the one that ordered, so someone would be getting a free meal. The final possible outcome being that the driver completely gives up and leaves the order at a random address if it's been paid for and leaves, thus stopping the customer from getting their food anyway.

All of these can be avoided by simply answering your phone after you make a delivery order. That is the simplest, and easiest way to avoid said situations coming to the fore.

**Be patient and attentive to questions.** While this should be generally accepted, it is truly one of the biggest problems in delivery. Many time people will give their address and not think twice about how difficult it might be to find their home. As such, what should only be a ten m,inute delivery turns into forty-five minutes while the driver tried to contact the customer for clarification, or they call the store to try and get the customer to answer and clarify just where they are going.

Be warned, if the delivery driver cannot find your residence and cannot reach you, the likelihood that you will receive your order is small. Most companies with delivery service have a policy that no order should leave the store more than twice in one day. Anything beyond that is a waste of time, effort, and money. As such, those orders can be marked as consistent pranks and removed from the delivery system fairly rapidly. In order to avoid this, be specific and answer any questions the person taking your order or the driver may have with you on the phone. Specific and correct details will save you a lot of time and effort in the long run.

**Do not expect a delivery driver to meet you in an area flooded with people.** There have been multiple horror stories on the internet and the evening news alike that outline incidents where a person is jumped or assaulted after being surrounded by multiple unknown people. For delivery drivers, they are taught to avoid any situation that could lead to this every single time they go out on the road. As such, if they pull up to an address and see a group of eight to ten people outside the likelihood of them exiting their vehicle is slim. Most drivers are encouraged to call their customer and let them know they have arrived or are in the area. Especially if they notice a large crowd of people around the home.

More often then not, a scenario where there is a large crowd of people is benign. However, that one chance in a thousand that it's not, is still too much of a risk. Most managers will tell that driver to bring the order back as soon as possible if that is the case. So to avoid this, be prepared to come out and meet your driver away from the crowd, or to answer their phone call so you know they have arrived and other plans can be made.

**If you are having food delivered to a public place or work, make sure you give specific instructions on where the order is to be placed or delivered.** Believe it or not, this is one of the highest reasons for returned deliveries. More often than not, people will order food to their place of work or a public place, but no instruction on how to actually deliver it. The problem with this, is a high traffic area, leaves more chance for others to intervene and essentially rob a delivery driver of their order.

More than that, without an accurate phone number with which to contact you, they cannot confirm the order is real or not. When this happens, the order is taken back to the store and slotted away as a possible prank. Leaving you without your lunch and the driver leery because they were sent into a situation that was more than a little questionable. Fixing these issues takes a lot of time, and definitely brings a serious amount of frustrations to both parties. However, it is a hope that these new guidelines given will make everyone aware of how these situations can be avoided so no one mistakes a delivery for a robbery set up, or why some deliveries would look that way.

Be that as it may, when and if such a situation occurs, give the individual committing the robbery whatever that ask for. Do not try to be a hero. Just give them what they ask for and stay out of their way. No matter what anyone says - your boss, your friends, your co-workers, the customer: do whatever it takes to keep yourself as safe as possible. After all, things and objects can be replaced. People, not so much. So do everything in your power to keep everyone as safe as possible.

# CHAPTER 21
# SCAMMERS BEWARE!

This chapter will be a long one, as we are covering a very important subject in the customer service world. Each of these situations have their own unique flair and will be something you encounter on more than one occasion. With that in mind we will start with the most extensive of the subjects in the customer service world: Scammers.

Scammers are exactly that. People who use whatever loopholes or means necessary to acquire free items or foods based on their knowledge of how a business runs. It is important to remember, that with the advance of technology keeping track of orders that have issues, a person who is set on the path to scam people and businesses out of money, do their research. They will use any and every means necessary to enact their scheme, so you have to be vigilant and know or recognize them by name, address, or even appearance. These are things that are not easily accomplished. That said, their choice of scam, once you learn it, is very recognizable.

The first example for the scammer that we will use, comes straight out of the food service industry. Pizza joints across the nation are known for their policies, even on food they deliver. The adage, 'the customer is always right' is one that people like to abuse in profound ways. If an order is wrong, you want to be sure the customer gets what they pay for, however, some abuse that knowledge. This scam is one called "the leftover."

**Employee:** Thank you for calling, [insert name here]. How may I help you?
**Felicia:** Yes, I'd like to place a delivery order.
**Employee:** Yes, ma'am. May I get your phone number, name, and address.
**Felicia:** My phone number is 555-011-1256. My name is Felicia Adams and I live at 123 Cherry Street.

Typing in the information given, it is clear the customer has ordered here before. Knowing they are in the delivery area, the conversation continues.

**Employee:** Yes, ma'am. Thank you. What can I get for you this evening.
**Felicia:** I want a medium pan pizza. No original sauce. I want the garlic parm sauce, cheese, black olives and pineapples on one half.
**Employee:** Alright, so I have a pan pizza, no original sauce. Garlic parm, black olives and pineapples. Would you like anything else with your order today like cinnamon bites or a cold, refreshing drink?
**Felicia:** Let me get an order of your garlic knots and an order of cinnamon bites.
**Employee:** Yes, ma'am. I have a Medium Pan, no original sauce, with garlic parm, black olives, and pineapples. An order of cinnamon bites and an order of garlic knots. Will this complete your order?

**Felicia:** Yes. What's the total?

**Employee:** Your total is 28.27. Would you like to pay with cash or card?

**Felicia:** Card.

Seems innocuous enough, right? The card number is taken and once processed the order is sent back to the kitchen. The food is prepared and sent out for delivery. All seems well with the world and the shift continues. Until an hour later when the phone rings.

**Employee:** Thank you for calling, [insert name here]. How may I help you?

**Felicia:** I placed an order for delivery and my food is wrong. Can I speak to the manager please.

**Employee:** Yes, Ma'am. Just one moment.

The employee goes to find the manager on shift. Explaining a customer is calling with a complaint, the manager makes their way to the phone to get the situation handled.

**Manager:** Thank you for calling, this is Marie speaking, how may I help you?

**Felicia:** I called earlier and placed a delivery order. This pizza is not what I asked or paid for.

**Manager:** I do apologize, what seems to be the problem?

**Felicia:** Yes, I ordered a thin crust with no original sauce, garlic parm, black olives, and pineapple.

**Manager:** I see. Give me just one moment.

The manager then puts the customer on hold and starts using the information they have from the caller ID and the description of the order to find the ticket in the system. They pull the employee aside and asked what happened, they swear that they took the order as it was given. Still, it's your job to keep the customer happy, and it's possible that the employee misheard the customer. It is pretty loud at rush, so it is a possibility.

Getting back on the phone, the Manager begins the conversation again.

**Manager:** Miss Felicia, I do apologize. I pulled up your order and I see they rang you up for a pan. You said you wanted that thin crust?

**Felicia:** Yes, Ma'am. That is what I asked for, my kids don't like all that bread.

**Manager:** I do understand. Again, I'm sorry and what I will do is send out a remake for your pizza, this time as a thin. Since we messed up your order, would you like a soda for the inconvenience?

**Felicia:** Thank you so much, and yes. Do you have Mountain Dew?

**Manager:** Yes, Ma'am. We do. I'll get this pizza remade and sent out with your drink. Again, I do apologize for the mix-up. You should see your delivery in about twenty-five to thirty-five minutes.

**Felicia:** Thank you.

**Manager:** Yes, Ma'am. You're welcome. Have a nice evening.

The phone is hung up and the new order goes through. The night progresses and the newly made delivery heads out to correct the mistake. Once again, the driver returns and all is well for about twenty minutes. Then the phone rings again. The employee answers and once more has to go find a manager.

**Employee:** There is a complaint call on line one. They are asking to speak to a manager again.

**Manager:** Alright.

Despite anything else taking place, the manager makes there way to the front and get back on the phone.

**Manager:** Thank you for calling, [ insert name here]. This is Marie speaking, how may I help you?

**Felicia:** I just got my remade pizza and this is not what I asked for. I wanted a Medium Hand-tossed pizza, no original sauce, with garlic parm, black olives, and pineapple.

The manager pauses, she was the one who rang up the remake. She knows for a fact that the customer had asked her for a thin to replace the pan. There was no way she misheard. However, arguing with a customer is not permissible, so she has to try and navigate the matter more easily.

**Manager:** I...see. Well, I do apologize that the pizza is wrong. I can send a medium hand-tossed to you. It will be another wait for about thirty minutes, but I can have it out to you just as quickly as possible.

**Felicia:** My kids are up late waiting for their food. What are you going to give me for the trouble.

**Manager:** Again, I do apologize. I am more than happy to remake the pizza and send out an order of cinnamon b-

**Felicia:** - *cutting off the manager* - I already have cinnamon bites. What else do you have.

**Manager:** Well, other than that and the drink I can offer you bread sticks or cheese sticks.

**Felicia:** I will take the cheese sticks. Try and get it right this time. - *Hangs up* -

The manager then rings up the third order. This time, to make sure there is no issue, Marie makes the whole of the order herself. This time, she takes pictures of the food as it comes out, and a picture of the three receipts from all the orders that were made and sent to this address. Keep in mind, only the first order was paid. So the two since, were sent to the customer free of charge, and cost money for the preparation, the delivery, and the product used.

The new delivery goes out, and Marie returns to working the floor. Again, all is quiet as the store begins to wind down for the evening. Everyone begins to start clean-up, well as much cleaning as they can get done while still having a functioning kitchen. The driver returns and begins their part of the cleaning, when the phone rings yet again. For the third time in as many hours, the employee calls for the manager to come to the phone.

As Marie approached the employee explains that it is again, the customer who had a problem with their order. This time saying there wasn't enough sauce on their pizza. This particular franchise, has a limit policy on the number of remakes that can go out to an address in a single shift. Today, the customer has reached the limit of that amount of deliveries for a mistake. So, Marie must now speak to the customer and explain there can not be another remake.

**Manager:** Thank you for calling, [Insert Name here]. This is Marie speaking, how can I help you?
**Felicia:** I asked for a pizza with garlic parm, and there is not enough sauce on here. The pizza is burnt, and we can't eat this. I want another one.
**Manager:** Ma'am, I understand your frustration, but sadly, I regret to inform you that I cannot send another order to you this evening. I will be more than happy to forward your name and number to my store manager...
**Felicia:** I want my money back. You're telling me you refuse to send me what I paid for?
**Manager:** No, Ma'am. I am not allowed to send out another delivery because there has been such a problem. I am more than happy to remake it if you want to come up here. Or you can speak with my store manager to-
**Felicia:** - *Cutting off the Manager once more* – If I could drive to the store to pick it up, I would not have ordered delivery. I want a refund.
**Manager:** Yes, Ma'am. I understand. I do apologize for the troub -

**Felicia:** Just give me my refund. You can bet I'm going to lodge a complaint. What is your name?

**Manger:** Marie, ma'am.

**Felicia:** And your bosses name?

**Manager:** Her name is Healani.

**Felicia:** I'll be talking to her and her boss tomorrow.

**Manager:** Yes, Ma'am. Again I do apologize. You're refund has been returned to your card. I do hope...

**Felicia:** *-Hangs up the phone -*

Now, for the scam. Indeed, the next day, Felicia calls the store and talks to the Store Manager. Said Manager makes a pizza and sends it out, and thus it is believed the situation is over. Until two weeks later. An internet order that is the exact same as the first order comes in. A delivery that is made and sent out. But it starts the exact same string of events. This time however, the first order had been free due to an online coupon.

Again, Marie is the manager on duty and when the calls come in to complain, she is the one that handles them. This time however, there is no money refund to handle. This night ends the same as before, with Felicia threatening to call the store manager the next day.

This time, Marie and Healani look into the customer's order history. They find that in the last six months, every time that Felicia ordered there have been multiple remakes sent out. More than that, almost each order had a refund when she did pay. After those orders, she would put in a delivery order online for free. Come to find out, she was filing complaints with the corporate office to get free pizza coupons and then complaining on them as well.

When one looked into the cost of the freed out orders, the delivery fees, and all other attached costs, she had gotten over seven hundred and fifty dollars in free food in just under six months. The scam, was simple...you continue to complain and use the customer service aspect of the business to get remakes delivered, and then complain to corporate in order to continue eating for free. The plan was a good one, especially when you used the free pizza coupons from corporate online so no one would be the wiser.

However, when you piece the whole thing together by deep diving, it outlines a huge loss of money, time, and profit. When that information was turned over to the corporate office, Felicia was removed from the customer base and blocked from ordering at any of the franchise stores in the area around her. The scam, while genius, was extremely costly. Effective while it went undetected, but something that eventually would have caught someone's notice. For sure, she had a lot of left0overs and food to tie her over until the next time she needed to order when she would start the whole act again.

This is only one example of a scam you will encounter. There are tons that float around, not just in food service but in retail as well. The point being, while it may be tedious, it pays to look into every complaint you get. It helps to avoid situations like this where your staff, your store, or your company will bleed money. The faster you find them, and the faster you learn to detect the line for excessive misuse of the system, the easier your job will become.

## CHAPTER 22
## TALK IS CHEAP

There is a lot of things in this world that cost you an arm and a leg. One thing that doesn't is conversation. The title of this chapter could be a little misleading though. Talk is cheap, is not meant in a derogatory way. Instead, it's a creed that should be applied to the service industry en masse.

Why?

To answer simply, conversation with your customer, employee, or boss is free. Simple words, and how they are spoken can set the stage for how an interaction or even a whole shift will play out. More than that, you can be the key point in changing someone's day or experience with just the words spoken with someone else.

Talk is cheap. Words are the easiest thing to give. We speak them everyday, from the time we wake up, to the time we go back to sleep. For some, even in sleep words are given to the world at large. It costs nothing to look at someone and say a simple 'Hello' or 'Good day'. Talk or communication, as it were, is the one thing that does not cost a person a dime.

When you work in customer service, it is your job to make the customer feel welcome. Many people believe, just calling out the generic greeting that the company you work for offers would be enough. Yet, it's the employee that calls them by name that garners the most reaction. The reason is simple, people just want to feel like they matter.

So, this chapter is meant for all of us. Customer, Worker, Rich, Poor, whatever you may be - we all just want to be seen for who we are. In the end, no one wants to be defined by what they wear, or the job they work, or their haircut. People want to know that you see them as the individual they are.

While some may believe this chapter to be waxing poetic or philosophical, in truth, it is the one lesson that anyone working in, or shopping to be part of customer service, we all just want to be seen. Acknowledged and noticed as the person we are and not the circumstances around us. Everyone wants to be treated in the same way, well.... mostly everyone. There are always exceptions, but that is not what this chapter is about.

It's about talking to one another instead of making everything a contest. Or a judgment. If you are a customer service worker, instead of huffing or rolling your eyes when a customer asks a question, answer them by asking what exactly they are interested in. Learn about them. If you are a customer, don't get impatient with the counter worker that nervously fumbles with the keys to punch in your order. Instead, take a breath, smile and ask their name. Put the worker at ease and watch them relax enough to put in your order.

A few...simple...words.

They can create the biggest changes almost immediately.

How many times would a situation you were in have easily been solved by someone saying, 'Let's take a minute.' Don't we all have a moment that we wish we had said something differently then what we did? Would we have even been in those situations if instead of saying something in the heat of the moment, we had instead taken a breath and said something less aggressive?

Sadly, we are fallible and humans make mistakes. We are emotional beings that act out and react to the world around us. Yet, one person nearby to say a kind word can make us loose our bluster and the winds calm. A reflection of ourselves that makes us think again about what we were doing just a moment before. Which is why offering simple words or actions can shift the tide of an encounter around us.

If you work in customer service and a customer comes at you yelling, instead of squaring your shoulders and setting your jaw, change the mood. Listen to them scream and then just say, 'I am sorry your upset, let me get your name and help fix this for you.' This approach is a lot more apt to get the customer to calm down then if you were to glare at them and then talk to them curtly by saying, 'And what was the name on the order?' Most times, the second phrasing makes the returning customer even more livid. Some take it to mean you think they're lying, others think you're annoyed with them and hate being made to feel like they are a pest. Which in turn escalates the situation.

Using that first phrase though, more often then not, will garner a different reaction. Speaking to the customer and taking the time to learn their name while you solve their problem goes a long way to making them feel that they are noticed. That you legitimately see them as a person and want to fix things for them.

Again, words are easily given and free to offer to completely change the tone of a situation. So keep that in mind. No matter which side of customer service you are on, you can change the tone of any situation you happen to come across by thinking about what words you will say.

## CHAPTER 23
## UP-SELLING REQUIRED

Working in customer service, or being a patron of one of these places, there is one necessary evil we have not discussed. Up-selling.

While it is not something that anyone wants to deal with, it is something customers have to hear and that service workers have to offer. While many think it is pedantic and unnecessary, it should be remembered that these companies are all about one thing, the bottom line. Money. The Green. The Root of all Evil.

Up-selling is the only way that these companies can be sure that their employees are trying to maximize profit. Worse, employees have to offer what they are told, because nowadays, every phone call is monitored and can be pulled up by the company to listen to. Some of these businesses, even employ secret shoppers to call on the phone and critique their calls. If you do not up-sell, or offer what you are told, you get a write up.

If you are a customer you have to listen to this worker offer you things that you don't want. However, some of these things are meant to be trigger words to try and entice you to buy these extras. Much like…when you go to a certain burger franchise and order a burger and they ask, 'Would you like Fries With That?'

This particular practice has become front and center at about any restaurant or customer service oriented business. It is a part of running in a capitalist economy. Which is why this chapter is going to be relatively small.

There is literally nothing to say about up-selling other than, be patient with one another. I promise you, the customer service worker doesn't want to have to offer those extra items as much as you don't want to hear about them. So let the scenario play out as it may. Have patience while getting through that portion of the conversation.

Much as I wish I could tell you that you could make up-selling disappear, I fear that is something which will never happen. This practice is something that has spread like wildfire. The results of which, caused enough of a bump in profit that it is now mandatory and encouraged daily. As unwelcome as it may be, upselling is now a necessary evil in the service industry, so learning to accept it and go with the flow is the best we can do in handling it.

# CHAPTER 24
# VALERIE VIXEN

The next personality to touch base on is one that we have all known. The Valerie Vixen is exactly what it sounds like. Shallow, I know. Sadly, there is always one person that is attractive and knows it. Whether from the strictures of society, or their upbringing, these individuals believe their inherent prettiness is a commodity to be traded on.

The Valerie Vixen, no matter their gender, is vapid. Not in a simple, glance at a mirror or reflective surface and adjust hair every few minutes, but truly shallow. Most these individuals have the depth of a drop of water underneath a boulder. Any situation that these individuals find themselves in, they think their appearance is a blessing to all and as such, should be rewarded with whatever they ask for.

It is not uncommon for them to smile and flirt in an attempt to stupefy the person and get whatever it is they ask for. Honestly, it is akin to seeing Poison Ivy use her toxin on unsuspecting members of Gotham to get them to do their bidding. The funniest part, is when reality sets in and someone shuts that show down fast. You never really know which way it will go until you witness it.

Admittedly, the successes are almost as funny as the failures. Mostly because, when you see someone fall for it, you cannot help but shake your head and then pull them aside to clarify what they just allowed to happen. So of course, we have an example:

Normal day, and a female walks in wearing a pair of designer jeans that fit like a second skin with a nice, ruffled blouse. The blouse is a dark jade color that seems perfect to accent the woman's skin tone. She has long dark hair, and bright green eyes as she walks through the door of the store. The male employee standing at the front counter gulps, his eyes trained fully on the female as she makes her way to the counter, offering him a bright smile before she speaks.

**Vixen**: I'm here to pick up an order for Valerie.

**Employee**: Um...uh...yeah. Um... I have that... right here.

The employee checks the computer, sees that the order is already paid for, so moves to gather everything that was to accompany the order. Bagging and boxing it up, the employee takes it to the counter setting it in front of her.

**Employee:** Well, I have two pizzas, sticks and a cake. You have a two liter coke and two marinara dipping cups. Thank you for choosing Pizza City.

**Vixen**: I don't get icing for my cake?

Now, Valerie deploys her secret weapon. Her eyelashes flutter, her head goes down, and her lip sticks out in a pout as she looks to the employee.

**Employee**: Uh... Uhm.... Sure.

He smiles bright, head tilting as he leans over grabbing the cup of icing to plop down on top of her order as she pushes it towards her. Valerie has scored a direct hit, and now one can only watch as the employee becomes a drooling mass of hormones.

**Vixen**: My Garlic Butters are in the boxes?

Again, a flutter of eyelashes as Valerie leans forward at the counter. The employee, staring none to shyly giving a weak smile.

**Employee**: Mmm... Uhm.... How many do you want?

**Vixen**: We needed three.

Once again, you watch as the employee moves to grab three cups of garlic and dropping them down on the boxes. Vixen smiles, nodding a little as she picks up her order and turns to head out the door.

The employee stands there staring after her, starry eyed as she makes her escape. Honestly, the execution by a Valerie is impressive. In the space of a few moments, you saw her eyes a target, zero in, and blow them completely out of the water leaving pure decimation in its wake. Once she has left the building, you are left having to explain to this employee that they now owe the store money for the extras they have given the Vixen. Many do not realize just how big a problem it is until it happens.

That said, one cannot help but appreciate the ingenuity of the female in getting the items she wanted. However, morally one has to object since doing so is the equivalent of stealing since she did not pay for those items like everyone else. This is why I say it is amusing to see the ploy of a Valerie Vixen work. Mostly because, it will only work once. If these it anything people understand, it's money. So losing any of your hard-earned pay on a woman whose name you don't even know, is kind of galling.

That said, the bombing of a Valerie Vixen in their pursuit of free goodies is hilarious. Mostly because those immune or now aware of her charms will make this situation so uncomfortable it's laughable. Which brings us to the example of that interaction.

This time, let's say that our Vixen is a tall male. Chiseled jaw, bright blue eyes, muscular build…you get the idea. He walks in the door and smiles at the female employee working the counter.

**Employee:** Welcome to Pizza City. How can I help you today?

**Vixen**: Here to pick up an order for Valerie.

Employee goes through the task of looking up the order, sees it is paid for and starts to gather the items for the order. Bringing them back to the counter while our male Vixen gives a small smile.

**Employee:** Here you go, two pizzas, a cake, an order of sticks, and a two liter coke.

**Vixen**: Really?

Vixen leans forward, tilting his head before letting his eyelids drop to give that smoldering bedroom eyes look.

**Vixen**: I don't get Icing for my cakes?

Here, is where the plan falls apart and the deviation in behavior is so abrupt that the situation becomes hilarious.

**Employee:** Sorry, but no. You can buy one for seventy cents if you would like to add it to your order.

Shock. That is the look on the Vixen's face. Their charms have not worked to enchant the person behind the counter for their free items. You can see the sheer panic, as they try and figure out if they have lost their touch, or if they just got caught trying to scam for free dipping cups. This is something they are not accustomed to, and could be a one off so now the gloves come off.

Our male Vixen leans forward, offering the employee a wink. His mouth curves up in a small smile as he speaks again.

**Vixen:** Are you sure? I can't get one just this once?

**Employee:** You can…if you pay seventy cents.

It is here that the train fully derails. The Vixen unsure of what is happening, begins to back away.

**Vixen:** Uh…umm…hmm….no, that's alright.

A tentative smile is offered before he moves to grab his food.

**Vixen:** My garlic cups are in with the pizzas.

**Employee:** There are no garlic cups, but if you would like some I can add them to your order. How many did you need today?
**Vixen:** You mean they aren't included?
**Employee:** No, Sir. They are also seventy cents a piece.
**Vixen:** I...um.... I see. No, I won't need garlic cups.
**Employee**: Have a nice day!

The male cannot get out of that store fast enough. Anyone watching cannot help laughing because you can see the confusion on the customer's face. Their wiles did not work and they think they are losing their touch. Or angry that they did not appeal to the person they were trying to flummox. To see them crash and burn is a horrible thing to revel in, but amusing none the less.

Being aware these personalities exist, makes you better able to handle them. Keep that in mind for the next time you come across a Vixen, whether at work, or the store, or just in general. These tips can save you a lot of time and money.

## CHAPTER 25
## WASHING MACHINE

This chapter is going to be more informative about the food service aspect of things. Mostly because it has been noted, people complain about what they consider sanitary or appropriate from food service workers, but not how their impatience makes some mistakes happen.

Thing is, it comes from not just customers, but other employees and management too. You would not believe how much time is lost everyday in having to repeat the same basic function or washing your hands. The worst part is people have no care or acknowledgment of making you walk away from what you are doing to facilitate doing it again. if anything, they are annoyed they have to wait on you while you repeat the whole process.

Washing our hands in food service is something we have to do every time we change tasks. Whether you are moving from food preparation, to food serving, or from taking an order on the phone to putting away stuff in a refrigerator – you have to wash your hands. This is why, most often in food service, once you wash your hands you try and stay in one spot, or one task. In a pizza place, if you wash your hands, you try not to move away from what is called the make line. The goal is to stay in one task so you do not have to wash your hands every five minutes.

However, what people do not seem to understand, is that when they walk in to the store or restaurant you work at and cannot be patient, they set a chain of events in motion that only ends up irritating them more. Especially on day shifts where there are fewer people available to work. When you have a customer who is demanding attention, it does not matter if you have greeted them and asked them politely to hold for a few moments, people ignore the obvious in front of them.

More than once, it has happened that a customer has entered an establishment with one person working the interior. The customer is greeted and told that they will be helped in a moment. The person working the interior is busily making the food and putting it in the oven in open view of said customer. Instead of waiting, the customer will walk over, away from the register and computer that is needed to put their order in and start yelling their order at the person making food.

At this point, the person trying to make the food is left no option but to stop what they are doing and move to the counter. Mind you, this customer need only look at the scene before them to realize that there is no one else. Food is coming out of the oven, the screen over the make line has lines of writing that are obviously orders as they have now stopped moving off the screen. Yet, they demand attention anyway.

The employee washes their hands, dries them, and then moves to the counter, punching in the necessary information to take the order that the customer was screaming over to them. The customer gets mad, annoyed that they are repeating themselves. Then annoyed further when they are told, it will take at least twenty minutes for their food to be ready, but possibly closer to thirty. They complain, making snarky comments at the front of the store, while the employee moves to wash their hands again. This time, after drying their hands they move to the end of the oven, removing the products that were coming out and boxing them up before putting them on a warmer.

They go back to the sink, washing their hands again, while the customer who was so rude continues to make snarky and snide comments. This is where the situation gets worse, because said customer will now eyeball your every move. They watch the employee begin to work on orders again, and the second they notice that the order being prepared is not theirs, the customer in question escalates the situation. They begin to harp on any and every small detail they can. Now the employee working has to stop yet again, and wash their hands to move to a place where they can address the customer.

That conversation typically goes like this:

**Employee:** Yes, Ma'am. How can I help you?

**Customer:** You aren't wearing gloves. Why aren't you wearing gloves to prepare food?

**Employee:** It is not required in this store or franchise ma'am.

To be clear, this is only true in certain food service jobs. Most pizza franchises, this is the case. Gloves SHOULD and MUST be worn for any food you prepare that is ready to eat – or goes straight to the customers mouth from being prepared. However, for actual pizza, they are not a requirement. The reason is that none of the food that is about to go through the oven is truly raw. No raw meats are used in pizza places. Even the chicken wings that you order were precooked and shipped, but require going through an oven or fryer at upwards of five hundred degrees. Therefore, there is no need for gloves in the preparation.

That does not stop people from complaining though. If anything it causes more complaints, but back to the conversation at hand.

**Customer:** What do you mean it's not required? I'm going to report you to the Health Department!

**Employee:** I understand that, ma'am. Our foods are not raw so we are not required to wear gloves. If you wish to report us, you are more than welcome to.

**Customer:** I will. Where is my order?

**Employee:** I still have to make it, ma'am. I came over to answer your question.

**Customer:** Why won't you make my food?
**Employee:** Ma'am, I am doing my best to get your food to you as quickly as possible.

The customer mutters and the employee walks away. Once more to the sink where they wash their hands. While there they notice that the time it took to speak with the customer saw the food put in the oven cooking and finished, so they dry their hands and once more pull items from the oven, box it up and place it on the warmer. They move to wash their hands again, just for the customer to get huffy again.

**Customer:** Why aren't you making my?
**Employee:** Ma'am, I'm trying.

This time, the employee goes straight to the make line and starts making the orders there. Of course the customer stands there, annoyed that it is taking so long for her order, but doesn't realize that her order came in after others on the screen. The employee rushes as fast as they can, finally making the food, and right before they have the last item in, the doorbell up front rings.

A second customer enters and moves towards the counter. Putting the last item in the oven, the employee turns and nods to the customer. Welcoming them to the store and asking for just a moment, before they move to wash their hands, dry them, and then move to the oven to catch the items coming out. Boxing them up and getting them set, they carry the orders to the warmer and proceed to the counter. Asking the second customer how they can be of service.

The customer states they are there to pick up their order. Information and money are exchanged, before the employee hands over the person's food. Meanwhile, the first customer starts shrieking about her food coming out of the oven.

The employee moves to the sink to wash their hands, while the customer begins her newest rant.
**Customer:** My food is about to fall. Go catch it!
**Employee:** Yes, Ma'am. I just have to wash my hands first.
**Customer:** Why are you taking so long?
**Employee:** Ma'am, I was just handling money I need to wash my hands before I go get your food.
**Customer:** I'm not going to wait for a remake because you messed up.

These situations are extremely frustrating. Admittedly, using a day shift with so little back up or help is the extreme, but this situation happens even when on a fully staffed night shift. A lot of people, even those working in the service industry, do not understand how difficult it is to have a situation like this one.

Knowing there is food to make and things to do, but every time you prep yourself and wash your hands, you have to do something different, can mean you wash your hands up to thirty times in an hour. It is not something to take lightly. There is a price to doing this so much. Using the soaps that are cleared for food service, they are abrasive to the skin and begin to dry it out, causing cracks, ridges and sores. The fingernails get weak and brittle.

So, the point of this whole long winded explanation, is this: Be mindful of what is taking place before you. With the workers and yourself, remember that trying to rush someone or make things go faster by pushing, can cause detrimental breaches in procedure. The last thing anyone would want is food made by someone who did not wash their hands after dealing with money or touching a computer. So try and be a little more patient.

## CHAPTER 26
## XENOMORPHS, PREDATORS, PENNYWISE, AND THINGS THAT GO BUMP IN THE NIGHT

Crazy chapter title, right? It's because this is the random, hodge podge that takes place in conversations throughout the world. Just because you are dealing with customer or food service, does not make any difference.

You will at some point have a random conversation about something genuinely non-work related while on the clock. Sometimes it will be with a customer. Other times it will be with another employee. Or, it may even be with your boss. The point is, it will happen.

These conversations can be a bright spot in the otherwise dreary passing of day to day life or work. They can be extremely entertaining, or thought provoking. The reason these are even being mentioned is because if we took the time to have more of these conversations with one another, the more mutual respect we would create among the populace.

These conversations can be spawned by a random thought or exclamation. A simple use of a phrase from a movie, or if one is so inclined a question that is posed from one employee to another. No matter what spawns the shift in topic, these conversations can be fun and enlightening to anyone taking part in them.

The example of one such conversation is one that took place not in a food service restaurant or a customer service store, but instead among a group of writers that were speaking on their own personal projects. These writers gathered together randomly week to week to discuss new and interesting ideas, video games, or even movies. So, as was typical, they began discussing the aspect of fear and villainy. Which brought us to a game of who would win, because the discussion had turned in that direction when it was learned that Sorcerer Mickey Mouse was able to defeat Jedi Master Yoda in a video game. (Outrageous, I know. I still debate that this was a mistake on the game makers part... because hello?! Yoda was so bad ass that he jumped UP ON DOOKU'S SHOULDER WHILE FIGHTING HIM. That little green Jedi was a monster... but I digress.)

So, the conversation continues with these writers pitting different fictional characters up against one another. For a while, they reached consensus in every single one that they posed to one another. Finally, they found the one question that to this day, remains a debate.

The question?

**Who would win in a fight, Pennywise or a Xenomorph?**

Now, to be fair, both of these creatures exist in two very different universes. However, the general rules of life, reality, and their abilities remains. For those of you not entirely clear on these two different characters, allow me to explain.

Pennywise is a villain in the Stephen King Universe. He is, in simple terms, an inter-dimensional being that thrives and derives his power from the fear of others. With this, he is able to create illusions, bend reality to what he wishes, and in general enact chaos in the world on a large scale. The limit of what Pennywise can do is something that does not exist. As long as he has a well of power to pull from, he can make anything one can imagine a reality. Therefore, he is in someways, unstoppable.

Xenomorphs, are the antagonist beasts of the Alien movie franchise. These creatures exist in the future of our reality, and use humans as incubators for their young. These creatures have an exoskeleton like one would see in insects, but far more durable. Their blood and saliva is acidic in nature, with the ability to burn through flesh, metal, and pretty much any kind of solid matter. Xenomorphs can move as both a quadrupedal creature or bipedal, with an extension of their tongue that is a hard, bone like shaft with a second pair of snapping jaws in their mouth. Lastly, these creatures have no eyes, but instead seem to use echolocation and a hive mind among their peers.

Here is where the question makes things a little gray. You see, Xenomorphs, are singularly focused. Find, conquer, and destroy. They do not fear anything before them. Not really. Their singular focus is their own survival, food, and procreation. While they try to save their own lives, because of the hive mind, they do not fear death. Instead, knowing others will take their place, they follow the collective almost exclusively. Because of this, they do not produce the emotion needed for Pennywise to have a well of power against them.

Pennywise, is fueled by fear, yet as an inter-dimensional evil, already has a well of power of his own. He is still able to shift and bend reality. Able to throw illusions and become whatever he needs to be in the circumstances.

The debate was an intense one. Some siding with Pennywise, others with Xenomorphs because of their ability to reproduce in the body of any being they infect. Never has a consensus been reached on this debate. However, the lively conversations it produced are more than enough to make it a worthy conversation piece for anyone, anywhere.

Admittedly, this random example does not illustrate the plethora of conversations that could randomly become a part of your day. There is any number of subjects that one could have to discuss.

Marvel, DC, TV Shows, Books, News, Star Wars, Star Trek, or any other number of things that people have an opinion of could be the center of conversation. There are only three subjects you want to avoid with all your might.

    Religion.

    Politics.

    Sex.

I underline these three because people seem to forget, that some subjects are not fit for random conversation. More than that, none of those three subjects define a person as who they are. Their likes, dislikes, or opinions on passing matters are insights to who they are more than these three subjects.

They are also the three subjects most likely to spark an argument in random fashion. So avoid them at all costs.

In the meantime, do not be afraid to strike up a conversation with the people around you. I promise it will be entertaining if nothing else.

## CHAPTER 27
## YEARLY RESET

One should take note that all businesses experience one thing every single year. The end of the fiscal year.

This time is when things transition not just for the company, but for the staff working at the store level. Numbers are crunched, studied and spit back out, meant to underline the things that need to change in the companies policies.

While many may think this does not affect them, in truth it does. At the end of this year, they do new program models to optimize profit by increasing prices, eliminating certain items from their offerings, and of course, labor. These year end financials are what cause things like a store becoming fully self-checkout. A restaurant no longer offering certain dishes. Then, the final nail in the coffin, staffing and cutting their labor cost to maximize profit.

These things while they do not appear to affect everyone directly, do in fact have an impact. These cuts in labor are why you can no longer call a store or pharmacy and get a person on the phone. They are also why when you do place an order at a restaurant for delivery you have to wait an hour and why no company still has a thirty minutes or less guarantee. In the end, everything trickles down then comes back, full circle.

It is important to understand that in these periods towards the end of the year you will find some inconsistencies. While they are bleeding off the items that will be discontinued, you will see a marked decrease in price. When you see this, buy as many as you can because it is likely you want see them again. While that's not what a whole lot of people want to hear, it is a sad truth.

While I wish there was a whole lot more information to give on this subject, the sad truth is, there is not much to stay. Only people at the corporate level can give you answers as to how they get the numbers they have and why they make the decisions they do.

The only reason I even attempted to make this chapter was because very few people knew this was actually a thing. I can tell you that the store level is where these changes hurt the most. So when you get frustrated with a lack of staffing or help, keep in mind these stores have no control of what they are being told to do. All they can do is follow the instructions they were given.

If you wish to know about these changes, you can try to talk to people in the corporate offices to try and get answers. Maybe you can affect the change needed. Otherwise, the best that can be done is to make people aware that the big changes they see in their favorite stores or restaurants comes from these end of year financials. To know they exist and make an impact.

So, be aware these happen. The fiscal year end is different from company to company. Although most companies aim for late November or early December in order to fall in line with national tax time. Most the changes instilled will take place around the New Year in order to transition the public through these changes as seamlessly as possible. So keep that in mind when something you normally acquire becomes unavailable around that time.

So, there you have it. Yearly Resets are something to be aware of, no matter where you may encounter them. As a customer, an employee, or a manager be prepared for these changes to roll out like clockwork every year.

# CHAPTER 28
## ZOOTOPIA

In the end, I suppose this book is more a list of guidelines instead of actual personalities of people for every chapter. The intent was just to make everyone aware of the situations around them in public settings where customer service is in play.

By no means is this a bible of absolute do's and don'ts. Instead it is the observations of someone who has seen, worked, and navigated the world of retail and food sales as both a customer and an employee. With this in mind, we have come to the end of our little survival guide.

At the end, humans are a pack animal. We have our structures and hierarchy in different social settings, but in the end, we all interact with one another in some way, shape, or form. The world is a great big zoo, and we are the animals on display. Our actions or in-actions, forming the entertainment for ourselves, and everyone around us.

Mankind is the most base of forms and will always be a pack animal. We follow and group together even at our most dire of circumstances. Despite caste or social level, we interact with one another in some form or way. Face to face, online, or in printed word, as a whole we remain in contact with others of our species spread out across a wide net of locations, status, or health.

The part we keep forgetting is that we are all human.

Everyone has their own struggles and problems. They differ from person to person, but they are there. These struggles exist and are very, very real.

So, going forward, remember that premise. If you do that, there will be less 'Karens' to discuss. Less eccentric personalities to have to manage.

The biggest point of this whole book: Respect.

Mutual respect for any and everyone, will go a long way to alleviating a lot of the issues we encounter. Treat others the way you want to be treated, whether you are the employee or the customer.

Learn to be kind but not a push over.

Learn to be patient with any and everyone because you never know why they are acting the way they are.

Learn to pay attention to more than your cell phone or your own issues. Look at the world around you, the people nearby, know they have their own obstacles.

In the end, customer service is a job that allows you to see people from all walks of life. The thing is, as a species, we should be serving each other.

Stop the useless belittling and arguing. Instead, try to lift others up and brighten their day. Do not pass judgment on these people around you and instead try and help them find an improvement to their situation, even if it is just a kind word.

You never know when you might be the one that makes the difference in a person's life. Even if you are just asking them, 'Would you like fries with that' wearing a smile.

## **About the Author**

Born in Fayetteville, NC Mariah Lynde found her passion for the world of fantasy in book at an early age. Spending many days with her nose buried in some written text rather than going out to play, it fostered her love of the written word. A military wife and mother of one, Mariah write from her home in the Piedmont of North Carolina. She is a former paramedic and an avid fan of Australian Shepherds.

## About the Publisher

Fae Corps is all about helping the Indie Author find the magic in their art. We are the authors and the small storytellers. We are all about helping the new and struggling authors to be seen. We are all about helping the indie author to find their voice. We believe in the indie author's magic to make a difference in this world.

Find Us at faecorpspublishing.org and our catalog is available at Books2read.com/rl/faecorpsllc